Byrd Nash

College Fae
Freshman

NEVER
DATE A SIREN

Copyright © 2019 Byrd Nash   www.ByrdNash.com
Cover Art by Original Book Cover Design
Publisher: Rook & Castle Press

ISBN 978-1-7334566-3-0
Library of Congress Control Number: 2019916273

Publisher's Cataloging-in-Publication Data
provided by Five Rainbows Cataloging Services

Names: Nash, Byrd, author.
Title: Never date a siren : a college fae magic series #1 /
   Byrd Nash.
Description: Tulsa, OK : Rook and Castle Press, 2019. |
   Series: College fae, bk. 1.
Identifiers: LCCN 2019916273 (print) | ISBN 978-1-7334566-4-7
   (paperback) | ISBN 978-1-7334566-3-0 (paperback) | ISBN
   978-1-7334566-0-9 (ebook) | ISBN 978-1-7334566-7-8
   (ebook)
Subjects: LCSH: College students--Fiction. | Magic--Fiction. |
   Fairies--Fiction. | Sirens (Mythology)--Fiction. | Fantasy
   fiction. | Bildungsromans. | BISAC: FICTION / Fantasy /
   Contemporary. | FICTION / Fairy Tales, Folk Tales, Legends
   & Mythology. | FICTION / Coming of Age. | GSAFD:
   Fantasy fiction. | Bildungsromans.
Classification: LCC PS3614.A724 N48 2019 (print) |
   LCC PS3614.A724 (ebook) | DDC 813/.6--dc23.

You can make anything by writing
C.S. Lewis

Dedications

To my Honey Bee
La vie est une fleur dont l'amour est le miel.
Victor Hugo

To my Eldest
who inspired much of Logan

Freshmen Year, Spring Semester
Leopold-Ottos-Universität
Geheimetür
Bewachterberg

Chapter One
Room Needed

Brigit lost her apartment a week after midterms in the spring semester. It didn't help her grades or her mood.

"Look on the bright side," said Celia, "at least you won't have to deal with Sam's messes anymore."

"I'll be glad not to live with a pig, but he had no right to throw me out." At her angry statement, Celia reminded Brigit of her warning about getting involved with the temperamental Sam in the first place.

"I told you when you refused to sign that lease you'd have no recourse if things went poorly. And with Sam, they were bound to go poorly."

Brigit didn't tell Celia the reason she hadn't signed

the lease was it required a background check. As it was, the freshman had already lied about several things on the college application she had submitted last fall to the Leopold Otto University in Geheimetür.

Leopold Otto was the only higher learning institution in the human lands even willing to admit the troublesome fae to their program. Indeed, the country of Bewachterberg was friendly to her kind because of the Treaty of Sigismund. But Brigit, with the suspicious and skeptical traits native to the fae, knew welcomes could be withdrawn.

Not willing to discuss the apartment lease any further, Brigit dipped a spoon into some of the cheesy Spätzle from Celia's plate and ate it while looking about the hall. The two students were seated in the university's main cafeteria, a building over 400 years old which once had been the infirmary of the original monastery building complex. Brigit loved the soaring ceilings, the exposed ancient wooden beams, and the floor-to-ceiling coffered wall paneling.

The aged wood gave the dryad pleasant shivers.

"You'll just have to find another roommate," scolded Celia. "Before you ask, you can't sleep on my couch. I already have three squatting in a two-bed apartment with only one bathroom. As it is I'm about ready to kick out Katey's free-loading boyfriend."

Brigit sighed and ran a hand over her forehead,

causing tight black curls to briefly pull back from her face, revealing deep brown, almost black eyes. Like many of the fae, she was thin. It gave her a deceptive appearance of frailty; in reality, she was twice as strong as a human of the same outward appearance.

"I can't sleep in the library one more night with those ghosts. I guess after you die, you give up any sort of decency."

Celia pursed her lips, leaning back into her chair, as she considered Brigit's problem. She was a curvy woman with long, curly chestnut hair, a friendly countenance that held sea-green-blue eyes, and a mild smile.

The two fae had met during the last semester and had bonded over several things: they were both of the fae Sept, or clan, of naturals as Brigit was a dryad and Celia a naiad, and they had despised the biology professor teaching the class they shared.

The dining tables in the hall were filling up with students. Celia's eyes found a target, and she leaned over to tell Brigit, "What about that guy? Stop. Don't look yet. Yeah, he's seated now."

The nursing student dropped a napkin off the side of the table and gave an expressive sideways glance to where it fell to her friend. Brigit pushed her seat back and bent to pick it up, taking a casual look under her arm in the direction where her companion had indicated.

3

A male human with dark hair was seated two tables over by himself. He was looking through a textbook while ignoring the Gulasch before him.

"Him? What about him?"

"I hear he has a two-bed apartment. Very nice. One of those new downtown lofts. Roomy. I bet it has lots of windows, unlike Sam's cave dwelling."

"How would you know about it? Been inside?"

"He visited the dispensary during my rotation, and we chatted. He's here as an exchange student. The university is so desperate for money they let him bend the rules and room off-campus. The grapevine says he's from a stinking rich American family, so I bet there's no week's worth of instant noodles in his pantry cabinet."

"But he's a human, Ceel," protested Brigit. Last fall was the first time she had been around humans since leaving the Perilous Realm. They still disconcerted her; their energy fields weren't exactly unpleasant, just strange. Brigit had not struck up any relationships with them yet and wasn't sure she would.

"It'd be weird. I've never shared with a human before."

"At least go look it over. Never hurts to know what's out there."

When the young man finished his meal and left his table, Celia made hand gestures encouraging Brigit to

4

follow him. Without an alternative solution, Brigit grabbed her backpack and swung it over her shoulder.

Tracking him, Brigit was careful to stay far enough back, blending into clusters of human and fae students as she traversed the quad of the university. This part of the campus was the oldest area of Leopold Otto. The ancient buildings from the original monastery stood almost untouched, and the grand oaks made for a majestic parkland.

It was her favorite part of the campus despite the disconcerting habit of humans unaware they were walking through the ethereal bodies of Benedictine monks. You'd think they would give their own people respect. But it was just one of many things that Brigit found confusing about her fellow students.

Even though she lost sight of the human, Brigit had no fear she'd miss him. Like all beings from the Perilous Realm, she had the ability, now that she had marked him, to feel his energy trail. He wouldn't be able to escape as long as she kept her intent focused.

At the corner of the campus, she found him standing at the bus stop for a downtown route. The buses were the best way to travel throughout Geheimetür. The city restricted motor vehicle access, permitting only electric trolleys, scooters, and bicycles to enter the historic market center area.

When the electric bus quietly rolled up, it was easy for her to become part of the crowd. Flashing her student ID at the driver, Brigit quickly made her way down the aisle. She passed him without making eye contact and grabbed a seat near a window.

The bus doors shut and the vehicle pulled forward. From behind the shelter of her book, the dryad surreptitiously observed her target: he wore a button-down, long-sleeved shirt, and khaki slacks. A bit formal for college life. Tall and lean, like a long-distance marathoner. He had thick, dark brown hair, almost black, that stood up like a haystack over his forehead.

The bus started to enter the old market town area of Geheimetür. Here Gothic and Baroque architecture stood side by side, acting as a physical timeline of Bewachterberg's past. As they continued the route, students, shoppers, and commuters got off the coach while Brigit's target remained seated.

Passing through the town center, they traveled through the former industrial area. Here the derelict factories, their purposes long extinct, were being converted under a strictly monitored urban renewal plan. Bit by bit, a swanky modern district with planned restaurants, shops, and apartments was emerging. Like anything that might disrupt the city's calm, Geheimetür tried to hide the construction by erecting fake temporary storefronts.

The student finally got off the bus, and Brigit watched him pass her window, seeing his face in profile before the bus pulled forward again. She waited for two more stops before hopping off herself. Circling the block, she came across the street to observe him mounting steps into a flat-faced, red brick building. While it was new, it mimicked the older construction on either side of it.

Brigit lightly touched the flowers and trees in the planters on the sidewalk. She greeted the plants as she edged herself closer to where the young man had entered.

"Beetle dung, a keypad," the dryad muttered under her breath as she saw her first real obstacle. "What do I do now?"

Generally, the fae weren't compatible with technology, though most managed to exist with it. However, Brigit's problem with communication tech was so significant the university had given her a disability waiver. Instead of a computer, she pounded out her class papers on an antique typewriter in the basement of the library. Lacking a mobile phone in the human lands was a big inconvenience, but it was a fact that cell phone batteries died if she touched them.

Brigit saw someone inside come to the front glass door, so she quickly skipped up the steps and grabbed the door before the guy exiting could shut it. Not looking back, Brigit made her way to the bank of elevators and made a show of pushing an "up" button.

By the time the elevator doors opened, the resident was no longer in view. Ignoring the elevator's open doors, she walked over to the end of the lobby. Standing in front of a row of mailboxes she dug into a pocket on her backpack.

She retrieved a pendulum with a stone carved from moss agate held on a silver chain. She let the stone warm up in her palm while she told it what was needed. Feeling its readiness to assist her, Brigit held the pendulum up to the row of numbers, moving it slowly in front of the mailboxes one at a time.

She had a bit of *Finder* in her fae bloodline, and the pendulum didn't fail her. It swayed harder in front of one particular box, indicating the apartment she wanted was on the third floor.

Knowing how lazy humans were, and disliking technology herself, the fae took the stairs to lessen the possibility of meeting someone. At each landing were small, narrow windows providing a bit of light and a potted plant squeezed into the corner. Brigit took a moment to give each plant a spark of her dryad energy. In her experience, indoor plants could always use a bit extra to keep them well.

She found apartment 305 at the end of the hall. In front of the door was a coco fiber welcome mat and since no one was in view, she knelt, and asked it, "Would you like to help me?"

I welcome people! Welcome. Hi! How are you?

It had a coarse, grating kind of voice in her head. Brigit's abilities let her communicate with organic material, whether it was living or not. She stroked the fibers with her fingers and palm, causing it to shiver under her hand.

"I need inside."

Help you! I'm a Helper! Wipe feet!

The palm situated at the dead-end of the hallway, just a few steps away, interrupted their conversation with a slight furry cough.

The man will leave in a moment with his laundry basket. I've heard the laundry is in the basement. I've never been there personally.

"Thanks."

Brigit formulated a quick plan, and after giving them instructions, she slipped back down the hall to the stairs. There she cracked the door slightly and took a seat on the top step in the stairwell. The freshman spent the time reading and highlighting a textbook to prepare for her chemistry test.

Engrossed in her work, Brigit missed the click of the apartment door. Luckily, the palm plant called out to her in its sonorous voice: *There he goes on schedule. I'm never wrong about my people.*

Peering through the slit between door and frame, she saw the human was waiting at the elevator, holding a basket of clothes against his hip. He had changed to a more casual outfit, now wearing a dark blue t-shirt and shorts. He seemed preoccupied as he at first didn't respond to the elevator ding. Only when the elevator doors started to close did he put out his hand to stop their motion and finally entered the lift.

Seeing him gone, Brigit crept out into the hallway and hustled back to his apartment door.

Welcome! Come in! Greetings!

Like she had requested, the doormat had edged itself over the threshold, a corner of it preventing the front door from closing and thus stopping the lock from engaging.

"What a good welcoming mat you are."

She wiped her feet across its rough fibers as thanks, and it wriggled in pleasure. Not forgetting to thank the palm plant, her fingertips stroked it, giving the chlorophyll cells in its waxy leaves a burst of stimulating, tingling energy.

At first hesitant to cross the threshold, when Brigit felt no barrier to admitting her kind, she stepped boldly into the apartment.

A short entry hall brought her past the galley kitchen. Curious, she stopped and poked her head into kitchen cabinets, where she found fast-food packets for salt, pepper, and a few bags of packaged noodles.

"So much for Celia's theory," Brigit huffed under her breath. Rich or not, he hadn't learned how to stock his shelves. She'd change that.

From the kitchen, she entered a living room with a sectional sofa, large screen television, and a sound system. The decor was masculine, with a lot of black, gray, and chrome. It was very trendy in a cold, impersonal way, but it was a style Brigit did not admire. That too would need to be improved.

"Needs plants. Rugs too."

The only thing of color or warmth was an open violin case sitting on a side table. Drawn to the beautiful lacquered wood, Brigit's hands hovered over it as she bent down to examine it more closely. The aged finish of the instrument had a beautiful patina that called for a caress, but the vibration emanating from it made Brigit hesitate. It felt like an ancient protection.

It was the only thing in the room she had encountered yet that had any protective shielding.

Not a good idea to be sticking your hand into a trap. Brigit did not begin a conversation with it, leaving the violin to continue her investigation.

The layout of the apartment included two bedrooms, each located on opposite sides of the living area. One bedroom had only a bed. Stacked on the mattress was a suitcase, unused sporting equipment, an ironing board, some clothes, and a pair of shoes.

The room had a connected bathroom with a sink,

toilet, and a shower that looked to have been unused for some time. Imagining a shower all to herself, Brigit did a dancing jig of excitement thinking of not having to use the changing rooms at the university's gym. Not only was the place cold, but the showers were often subject to sudden unpleasant changes in water pressure.

A sliding glass door led to its own screened patio. Looking through the glass doors, she saw a small apartment park with trees and a few benches.

Brigit sighed. This was just too good to be true. Why didn't this guy already have a roommate?

From the spare bedroom, the fae student crossed to the other side of the apartment. This bedroom suite had the same layout and a private bathroom. But this one was clearly in active use. The bed was unmade, the sheets rumpled, and the pillow showed that a head had rested there recently. At the night table was an alarm clock, a stack of spy thrillers, and a cell phone that Brigit avoided.

Not as cluttered as Sam's so the guy wasn't a total slob.

Brigit was just about to leave when she heard the mat cry out, *Welcome! Wipe your feet please!* and the turning of the front door lock.

What now? Brigit didn't have the invisibility powers of her other fae kin, possessing only a bit of look-away Glamour. She couldn't just stand here.

Impulsively, she dodged into the closet, pressing herself into the layers of clothes on hangers, and gently squeezing the hinged doors shut.

Ouch! Mind your elbows you scrawny twig!

"Shush," she warned the closet monster.

How dare you, you little upstart! I could eat you in one gulp.

Knowing the dangerous nature of these creatures, Brigit grabbed a finger and bent the digit back sharply, hissing, "Shut your piehole, or I'll give you something to cry about."

The monster gurgled, its thousand eyes bulging more than usual. Its mouth flapped open, revealing dozens of sharp spiky teeth in the little light coming through the split in the folding doors.

Do you always breathe so loud, fae twig? The human is not deaf.

The creature's rank breath blew onto her pointed ear, and Brigit gave him a sideways glare filled with acute dislike.

"If he opens this closet," she whispered back, "he'll be so busy mopping up what remains of you he won't have time for me."

She heard the human go into the bathroom and the sound of water running. Good, get in the shower and take a long, hot one that steams up the mirror.

Peering through the crack, Brigit saw the bathroom door reflected in the mirror over the dresser. He seemed busy. She slipped out to make her getaway.

"There's never a clean towel in here," a male voice cursed as he exited the bathroom. Brigit dropped to all fours, hidden from view because of the bed. To be on the safe side, she crawled to her belly and scooted underneath the frame.

Who do you think you are? This is my domain. Go find your own.

In the Perilous Realm, those who were not swift and decisive died. Without hesitation, Brigit poked the under-bed creature in its only eye with two stiff forefingers.

"Now be quiet, goon," she warned it.

The man's wet feet slapped over to the bedside. When he walked back to the shower, trailing a towel behind him, Brigit got an eyeful of his backside. Without clothes, his form showed to better advantage: long legs and torso, with narrow hips, broad shoulders, and a tight firm butt.

He might be human, but he was a good-looking one.

Hearing him busy in the shower, she edged out from under the bed to the sound of *good riddance* from under the bed and from the closet, *don't come back, twig.*

Brigit hurried out from the bedroom and was about to leave when the other room beckoned to her. Looking over her shoulder, she bit her lip in indecision.

Well, just another peek.

She slowly twisted the knob so it wouldn't make any noise and slipped inside the spare bedroom. After closing the door softly behind her, she sat down on the corner of the bed.

Sleep on us! The cotton sheets begged her, ready to fulfill their destiny. They were new and lonely.

"It isn't like he is using this room, right?" Brigit told the sheets.

Be our guest! We are here to embrace you!

It was a lovely bed and ready to extend hospitality.

Retrieving a pencil from her book bag, Brigit sketched a personal protective sigil on the flat wood surface of the door. The seal would give the room enough of a look-away Glamour that any human passing by would forget there was a door there. Making humans forget was well within her abilities.

Of course, it wasn't strong enough to work against a fellow fae, but it would do for a human.

Satisfied with her magic work, Brigit rubbed her hands, excited.

While it was a short-term solution, the idea of taking a shower and laying on clean sheets without listening to the harping nagging of ghosts made her giddy.

Chapter Two
Breaking Up is Hard to Do

L ogan waited in the doctor's office for his test results and found his eyes drawn again to the poster on the wall with the suicide hotline.

No, he told himself silently. No, everything would be okay. He was worn down from school; that was all. When the doctor returned he'd get some medication, and everything would return to normal.

The student health center attached to Leopold-Ottos-Universität was available to all students, regardless of their nationality. Even so, Logan's mother had insisted that he buy the school's health insurance policy if he was going to attend LOTTOS.

She also insisted on him renting an apartment off-campus, even though as a first-year student, this was unusual. She was not impressed by the small dorm rooms; spaces carved out of historical buildings. However, it all worked out in the end as dorm space was at a premium, so LOTTOS didn't make a fuss about him finding other accommodations.

That was how he ended up living across the ocean in a country no one from his home town had ever heard of. He couldn't blame them. He hadn't known of the place either until a letter in his senior year of high school arrived, inviting him to visit.

The hint of a scholarship as an exchange student was tempting. But when his cousin Evie, known for her uncanny predictions, told him he would meet the girl of his dreams Logan decided to go.

Flying into Paris and taking the train to Bewachterberg, he arrived at a place that seemed out of step with current times. The university's ancient buildings, formerly a monastery in the 1500s, and the quaint market town had all entranced him.

Seeing fae openly walking the streets seemed a fairytale come true. He found them alien and fascinating.

His first semester at LOTTOS had gone well. Logan was excited to return after the Christmas break to begin the spring semester when his new life crashed around him.

It was due to his girlfriend. An ex-girlfriend, he

corrected himself. Not exactly the girl of his dreams. Girl of his nightmares, more likely.

He had met Sibyl, a fae siren, when he was standing in line at administration to complete paperwork. The gorgeous blond girl with long hair and blue eyes like summer flowers stopped to talk with him. They shared a love for music, and within the first hour of their conversation, Logan believed Evie's prophecy had come true.

However, his mindless bliss of being in love lasted only for a few months. Returning in January, he immediately sought out his girlfriend, only to learn she was now living with someone else. He was stunned to discover he was well and truly dumped.

While mad about the injustice of how she treated him, Logan couldn't whip up the energy to feel much as he became depressed.

It was probably inevitable that his grades suffered as a result. As the weeks went by and the gray feeling intensified, Logan figured he better get a health check-up.

As it was, if he passed this semester, it would be a miracle.

Finally, the doctor returned, followed by a nurse intern. Recognizing the nurse as fae, Logan looked away, not wanting to make eye contact. He'd had enough of the fae for a while.

"You'll be happy to hear that all your test results are back. They are all normal."

"Normal?" asked Logan. That couldn't be right. He didn't feel right. "Are you sure?"

The doctor was a small, shriveled prune of a man. He looked over his reading glasses at Logan and back to the file folder and papers he held in his hands.

"Your blood and urine are normal," the doctor repeated, this time more loudly as if Logan was deaf. "Nothing to worry about. You're a healthy young man of twenty."

"But I have headaches. I've lost weight. I don't have any interest in eating. Maybe you should rerun those tests?"

"It's hard sometimes to adjust to a new place, far from family. Bewachterberg, especially Geheimetür, can be unsettling for newcomers. An adjustment period is expected."

He scribbled on a pad of paper and handed a prescription note to Logan.

"Nurse Rivers here will explain the medication. If you don't feel better in a few weeks, come back."

Logan opened his mouth to protest again, but the doctor left, closing the door behind him.

"I was sure I had mono, the flu, maybe a heart condition," muttered Logan under his breath as the fae woman sat on a stool next to a computer. She typed in a command, and the printer started ejecting printed instructions.

She turned to him and gave a professional smile with just enough concern that it did not to seem intrusively familiar.

"You did mention that you just broke up with your girlfriend this semester. The doctor has prescribed some anti-depressants to get you through it. We all have times when it's hard."

While he had fallen for Sibyl, it wasn't like she was the first girl he had ever dated or the first girl who had broken up with him. They usually left when they learned about his peculiar abilities.

"I've had breakups before. They've never given me nightmares, headaches, or impacted my will to live," said Logan with some acerbity. "Maybe because she was fae?"

"Fae?" asked the nurse, her eyebrows raised. "What type of fae?"

"I don't know. A siren is what she told me."

The nurse gave a look over her shoulder, back at the door, but it remained closed. She bent forward and said quietly, "Mr. Dannon, sirens are in the Sept of Beguilers, did you not know that?"

"No. And I don't know what that means. You might as well be talking a foreign language."

"A Sept is a clan. It's a classification that describes what type we are. For example, I'm a naiad, and I belong to the Sept of naturals. The Beguiler Sept is one well known for bespelling humans. Usually to the human's peril. Are you not a reader of the classics? *Argonautica* or *Odysseus?*"

"I'm an American. So not exactly."

"I'd recommend that you do some reading. The damage is done. Unless you can get her to release you, her spell will make you waste away, yearning for what you cannot have."

It took Logan a moment to realize that the irritating buzzing noise was his alarm clock. Flat on his back, staring at the ceiling, he wondered why the alarm. Wasn't today Saturday?

He flopped back onto the mattress, but the growling of his stomach reminded him he had forgotten to eat yesterday. He forced himself to roll out of bed to check the kitchen but the cabinets and fridge revealed nothing to eat. He had forgotten to get groceries again.

Logan was contemplating his next move when someone banged loudly on his front door. Before he could make it to the entryway, he heard the turning of a key. The college student gasped as it opened to reveal his least favorite person in the world: Sibyl, his former girlfriend.

"Oh, you're still here?" She asked, stroking back long golden tresses an achingly familiar gesture.

Despite himself, Logan felt a tug on his heart to touch her hair. Knowing that he was still under her siren's spell made him feel nauseated.

Intellectually, he found the siren a despicable being, heartless and cruel. Even knowing the truth, that the fae being had Beguiled him, he still yearned for those cloying kisses and possessive touches.

"I thought the orchestra had a rehearsal this morning?" She gestured her companion to come farther into the apartment as if she still lived there. "Franco Sabbatini, Logan Dannon."

"I know who he is," Logan finally spoke, crossing his arms so he wouldn't strangle Sibyl and her new lover. It still hurt remembering Sibyl's glee at explaining how she had upgraded from the third violin in the orchestra to the captain of the university's polo team.

Sibyl glided into the living area with the poise of a model on the runway. Casting a glance to the left of the room, she hesitated for a moment before turning to the right. Logan reluctantly walked behind her and Franco as they entered his bedroom.

"Sweetie, go get my boxes from the hallway," she commanded her new boyfriend. Franco complied with puppy-like enthusiasm. Logan felt bile in his throat; he had once been that guileless puppy.

The siren opened the closet, pulling out hangers, and throwing her garments across his bed. Boxing up her things had been one of the chores Logan had meant to do, but, like so many things, he had lacked the motivation to get it done.

Seeing Logan standing motionless, the fae commanded him to start folding her discarded clothes.

"I don't think so."

Her protuberant blue eyes locked with his own. He heard the whisper of wings and felt her power slide over him, her sharp claws digging into his heart so hard he gasped out a pained-filled exhalation. Being compelled, he found himself folding his ex-girlfriend's dresses, jeans, and shirts.

"That's a good boy," she said.

While she had forced him to comply, Logan still had some fight left. He sloppily folded the garments, throwing them casually into the boxes that Franco had brought back. Seeing his poor handiwork, Sibyl frowned.

"Let Franco do it. He's far better at everything, right sweetie?"

Angry but helpless, Logan thought again of turning to the university's Rector for help, but he discarded the idea. At LOTTOS, the Rector was in charge of running the university. When he had told Sibyl his threat she had only laughed. She dared him to do it and said if he filed a complaint, she would just Beguile the Rector too.

She knew that Logan was too particular about fair play. He would never permit his actions to cause another to come under her spell.

When Franco left with the last box, Sibyl stood in the living room, giving the area one last glance. She drew her hand over the bookshelf, her fingertips trailing lightly over his possessions.

"I told Franco what a fantastic apartment complex this is. He's looking into getting an apartment on the floor right above this one. We might be neighbors."

Her smile was toothy, and the points of her canines sharp and pointy.

"Did you ever love me?" Logan blurted out before he could stop himself.

At this question, she gave a fake, high laugh, playing at being human.

Why hadn't he seen through her act before?

"Of course I did, sweetie! Besides, that special talent of yours in knowing truth from falsehood would have warned you I was lying. So yes, I was head over heels in love with you, Scout's honor."

Sibyl gave that possessive, slow smile of hers that he had once thought meant she loved him.

"Truth detection has its limits. Remember, lover. You never asked what I loved. You never asked if I would remain faithful."

As she had explained so succinctly in their breakup

row, what she truly loved was her power over men. She had taken pleasure in telling him she was a shallow being, out only for conquests. He was a number on her scoreboard.

Logan couldn't help himself. It was like picking at a scab to see if the skin had healed underneath. He asked, "Wasn't one human heart enough for you?"

"I need fresh meat, love. It's what I do. Don't blame the cat for taking a mouse."

But siren spells didn't stop sarcastic replies, and Logan said, "Perhaps the mouse takes it personally."

"What can I say? It's just the price you'll pay for loving me."

The path of her hand had reached his violin, his most treasured possession. Her long, slender fingers hovered over the case, but she didn't quite touch it. She had always been obsessed with the musical instrument, a gift from his grandmother when he had turned twelve. But, despite her interest, she had never actually touched it.

Seeing Franco had returned, she gave him a broad smile. She rushed forward to squeeze her boyfriend's upper arm and her wet sloppy kiss caused Logan to turn away clenching his fists in frustration.

The couple started to leave, but the siren paused at the kitchen. Sibyl tossed a brass key onto the counter.

"I won't need this any longer."

She couldn't resist one last parting shot.

"It's too bad you missed rehearsal this morning. I wonder what maestro will say? You were lined up to be one of his favorites but probably not so much now."

Chapter Three
Balancing Act

B rigit woke up, stretching and yawning. She felt so good! No crick in her neck, no obnoxious ghosts to deal with it.

She smacked her gums and licked her teeth with her tongue. Ugh, fuzzy teeth!

She stood up and shook out her shoulders. Her clothes were a little wrinkled, but they were 100 percent cotton so, with a whisper of encouragement, they obligingly smoothed down at her touch.

In the bathroom, she pulled out a toothbrush and toothpaste from her backpack. After brushing, she rinsed out her toothbrush and set it by the sink.

Brigit decided she would be staying. The bed and

bath were just too good to go to waste. This guy didn't need the area, and she certainly could use it.

Occupying a room that a human didn't appreciate wouldn't cause that big of a debt. She could even justify it because tricking a human was part of a fae's birthright.

However, while Brigit could excuse away concealing her presence, she didn't feel it was right to live in the space without giving anything back. That pushed the limits of hospitality and the Laws of Civility.

The Laws of Civility were part of the Balance the fae kept. Any fae that did not maintain the Balance would be severely and swiftly dealt with by their kind. Knowing this, the human government of Bewachterberg let those from the Perilous Realm manage their own.

From an early age, Brigit learned any infraction to the Laws of Civility would disrupt the natural world. For every take, there was a give; for each obligation, payment in kind was expected; any insult was returned with an equal amount of force. The Balance was the only thing that kept the chaotic fae, numbering in the thousands of Septs, and hundreds of kingdoms, in check.

Brigit was meticulous about keeping her Balance in all ways. So even though her obligation was to a human, she would pay back the hospitality of having such a lovely room to call home.

Brigit thought over the problem while she worked on her hair. She had left a brownie at Sam's, and she was pretty sure that the fae being would love to move to a more agreeable situation.

Who wouldn't? Sam, being a troll, had little hygiene. The way he left his beard clippings in the sink and his hair in the tub always disgusted Brigit.

Undoubtedly, the brownie would love a better position.

Brownies were one of the few clans of the fae that worked closely with humans. They tended their homes, barns, or fields, to make all tidy and plentiful. If she could convince the brownie to housekeep for them, her roommate would be well compensated for Brigit's use of the room.

Thus the Balance would be maintained.

When her tight black curls made a perfect, angelic halo about her head, Brigit was satisfied. She struck a pose in the mirror, giving herself air guns, and a blessing chant to cheer herself to meet the day with the proper spirit.

"Oak, Thorn, and Ash. Time to dash."

Before leaving the room, she laid her palm on the door's sigil once more. Feeling the emptiness of the living spaces, she exited, backpack in hand. In passing, she noticed the violin and its case were gone.

Brigit was about to step out the door when a glint

31

of gold on the kitchen counter caught her fae attention. Like a magpie, she came closer. Inspecting it, she discovered it was only a brass key.

It wasn't her fault if humans were notoriously lackadaisical about doorways and physical boundaries. She scooped it up, murmuring with glee, "Finders Keepers."

At the front door, she confirmed again the coast was clear before exiting.

Yes, the key fit the front door just as she thought. Didn't she have the luck today?

Hello! Welcome, or is it goodbye? Are you leaving? He already left. When you come back I'll always be here for you! said the coco mat.

Brigit rubbed the mat with the sole of her shoes and gave a fondle to the hallway palm. The fae slid the key into her jean pocket and headed to the stairwell.

When Brigit discovered that the Treaty of Sigismund gave qualifying fae the ability to attend a human university in Bewachterberg, it encouraged her to implement a long-desired plan to leave the Perilous Realm. Using a long forgotten atlas from her parent's library, she discovered the location of a majestic, ancient oak. It was near the tennis courts of Leopold-Ottos-Universität and was a portal point.

Portals were specific gateways that could serve as a

bridge between the Perilous Realm and the human lands. One early morning she left home, using the tree to cross into Geheimetür. She promptly enrolled at LOTTOS as a student of botany and biology.

While she had been busy last semester adjusting to her new life in the human lands, Brigit never forgot her first friend. She always made a daily detour on campus to pay the matriarch tree respect.

Spring is almost near its end, said the oak.

"Finals will be here before you know it," Brigit agreed while laying her hand on its rough bark in greeting. The young fae closed her eyes, grounding and centering herself.

The forest sprite sent some healing to the tree's oak galls. This type of work took time and patience, and over the passing months, the two had come to know each other very well. She fed some of her energy downward, encouraging more of the oak's root hairs to sprout and grow, which would, in turn, help the tree get more food.

The fae breathed in through her nose and out through her mouth. Her emotions calmed as her thoughts merged with the heavy old ones of the tree where its tranquil nature combined with the sprite's more vibrant personality.

Brigit's heartbeat slowed as she fell into the tree's heartwood.

Blinking slowly she opened her eyes. She was inside

the portal now, surrounded by a gold-green light. The interior of the ancient tree held part of the Perilous Realm magic within it, making the area expansive.

As a dryad, Brigit had considered sleeping within the tree but knew it would be too risky. Anyone coming through the gateway would have found her immediately. Risking discovery was one reason she rarely used the portals between the Perilous and the human lands.

When Sam evicted her, Brigit had taken advantage of the oak's offer to store her belongings. Most of what Brigit possessed she had bought since starting school. There was little from home, but it was still all needed: clothing, textbooks, and notepads.

From one pile, she pulled out a work uniform, a green polo with the company name and logo embroidered in yellow on it. Her affinity for plants had landed the wood sprite a job within weeks working for a landscape and garden store.

Due to the Treaty of Sigismund, her tuition was gratis, but food and shelter were not. Even though it was her first time in the human lands, Brigit still understood Balance. Things weren't free, and there was always a price to pay.

Brigit kicked off her loafers, changed to clean socks, boots, and jeans. In fresh clothes, she hummed a tune as she crossed the threshold to return to Geheimetür. Patting the oak a goodbye she headed off to her usual stop, a corner bakery where she'd grab an orange juice and a blueberry muffin before heading into work for the mid-morning shift.

Working in a greenhouse was overall a fun, easy job for Brigit. The only potential hazard to her happiness was the chemical fertilizers. These she assiduously avoided by telling her employer she had an allergy, which wasn't far from the truth.

She enjoyed taking the early morning shift because it gave her time to commune with all the plants when humans weren't demanding she answer questions. Alone, she liked to pretend she was a mad scientist growing an army of minions. Grinning maniacally, arms upraised, she would shout "grow, children, grow, and we take the world!"

Automatic sprinklers maintained the larger greenhouses, but the flowering plants and bushes in the retail area needed support with daily visual checks. Being a Saturday, by lunch garden fanatics had wiped out quite a bit of stock.

Brigit tried to hide her frown of displeasure. She loved her job, but after the chemicals, it was people who were the problem.

And the weekends were the worst because more humans meant more questions. Wearing her work uniform, she couldn't avoid being seen by irritating people wanting things from her.

Because of her tiny size, barely five feet tall, she was often mistaken for a child or a young human teen until humans noticed the ears. Her slight frame also made humans think her incapable of carrying heavy sacks of soil and mulch. Their condescending remarks, cautioning her not to load their car for fear she would be injured, always irked her.

Another unpleasant aspect of interacting with humans was that because of her dark skin, Brigit sometimes received worse insults and remarks. Their racist epithets were infuriating, ridiculous, and inflammatory at all once.

She was fae first, and not a descendant of some human race, no matter what her appearance was. But given a racist insult, the dryad would stick a thorn from a Hawthorn tree in their vehicle's tires. Brigit maintained the Balance.

After a few hours of answering silly questions about what type of plants would grow best in their human gardens, Brigit retreated to the greenhouse located at the very back of the lot. Generally, she could rely upon it being a quiet green place - a spot for some breathing room from the Saturday shoppers.

However, as Brigit entered the last greenhouse, she found a fae being sitting on the side of a decorative fountain, playing with the Koi fish. The blond siren was Brigit's least favorite of the fae she had met at LOTTOS.

The hostility between them began when Sibyl tried to convince the dryad to join a club for the fae university students. Brigit's refusal seemed to be seen as a personal affront. The tension between them had continued to build so Brigit avoided meeting her on campus.

"I wish I could climb in there and join them," Sibyl told her. In an affected manner, the siren brought her long blond hair over her shoulder. The drape fell like a waterfall to her knees.

Her oval face, with its abnormally large blue eyes, and classical Greek features was just part of the facade the siren used to tempt humans foolish enough to believe such perfection was real. But her appearance could not sway her fellow fae. Brigit viewed her presence with irritation.

"Scat," said Brigit, wishing Sibyl was as easy to tame as a closet monster. "I don't need you seducing my boss."

Sibyl slipped off her sandals and put her long-toed feet into the fountain. Brigit ignored her antics. She had work to do.

Turning on the faucet, she took the hose and started watering the pots of bushes. Brigit was careful to keep herself farther than an arm's reach from the siren. It would be just like Sibyl to attempt some physical altercation if given a chance.

She was tempted to squirt the hose Sibyl's way but quelled the desire. The siren would insist on completing her dramatic performance one way or another.

"You haven't been attending our club meetings," said the siren, putting her chin in her hand as she observed the working dryad.

"Not this old song again," said Brigit, her irritation growing. "I have a full schedule, Sibyl, as I've told you numerous times."

"Really? Working for humans takes up that much time?"

"I need this paycheck. I don't live on thistledown like some."

Brigit wondered if Sibyl knew what a tactical error she had made coming to the dryad's domain. Because of Brigit's emotional turmoil, the plant life around them was becoming aroused. The rich smell of vegetation increased in the greenhouse as the plants connection to Brigit's emotions grew stronger.

A vine started creeping toward the siren wanting to fulfill Brigit's thoughts of strangling Sibyl. Brigit hushed its eagerness and tried to bring back the calm meditative feeling she had enjoyed with mother oak earlier in the day.

Finally, Sibyl came to the reason for her visit.

"I was at Logan's apartment this morning. When

did you move in? I didn't realize you knew him."

Beetle dung! So this guy Logan was the apartment's owner? Worse, Brigit hadn't realized her new roommate and Sibyl were connected. What a complication!

Pretending not to care, Brigit gave a noncommittal shrug. She found it a useful human gesture for many things.

Sibyl continued talking, her feet splashing the fish.

"Girl to girl, you should know that he's my territory and always will be. A siren never gives up her trophies. What is mine, stays mine, forever."

The siren's fatuous comment ended in a giggle. Brigit restrained the desire to punch her in the face, as the fae continued, "It's not like I even want him anymore, but I've got to keep my reputation intact. A siren marks a heart with a scar that can never heal."

"Who taught you that? Your mother?" Brigit sneered.

Everyone knew that sirens matured in a crèche. Not until a siren fledged did they gain human form. Maybe, being in animal form so early in a siren's development was why they missed social cues? Everyone knew that shapeshifters were odd in that way.

While the siren gave her trademark smile, as if unmoved by the insult, her hair shifted to the blue and green of peacock feathers, showing a lack of control.

"You are naive, Brigit Cullen, — if that is your real name. Strangely, I couldn't find you in any of the royal court records. And no one hereabouts even knew of you until you showed up last fall semester. Your college application seems pretty skimpy on details. For example, exactly which court do you owe allegiance too?"

"The kingdoms in the Perilous are numerous, Sibyl. Maybe you didn't look close enough?"

Brigit walked over and shut off the faucet. Doing so placed her further away from the siren. If Sibyl attacked, the dryad would have time to react.

"In one breath you insult me because I work a human job and in the next, you tell me not to date your ex."

Brigit's dark brown eyes had shifted to a rebellious black. She hadn't defied her parents and risked her Balance to have a bird-brained beauty boss her around. "I will manage my affairs, and you will stay out of my business."

"Logan is my business, so consider yourself warned, sprite."

Waving her hand like a beauty pageant queen, Sibyl walked away, leaving Brigit fuming.

Chapter Four
Bought Loyalty

Due to his exchange student status, Logan often received more attention than he desired. Of course, being late and stumbling in through the concert hall's door during the rehearsal of Dvořák's Symphony No. 9, didn't help anyone keep anonymity.

Logan was the third violin in the second violin section of a seventy-five member orchestra, so he reported first to the principal second violin mistress. Sadly looking him up and down, she administered a lecture about tardiness and letting down the ensemble. Sighing in disappointment, she sent him to the first violin concertmaster.

The concertmaster, a tall, bony man with the face of a passionate music lover, administered a blistering lecture to Logan.

The previous two sermons were only warm-ups for the Grand Slam delivered by the master. As instructed by the concertmaster, Logan waited while the maestro talked to various members of the orchestra. As members prepared to leave, they stopped to ask the maestro for advice or had information to give. Others came up to the conductor just for an excuse to glimpse the condemned man standing behind Kados Géza.

Eventually, though, all the orchestra members retired, leaving Logan alone with the maestro.

Kados Géza, the university's conductor, was Hungarian. Rumor was Géza arrived in Bewachterberg as a young child at the end of World War II. However, it was a mystery how he had managed this feat. From 1890 to 1989, Bewachterberg was concealed from the world through the power of fae magic and in this way, avoided both world wars and Russian occupation.

Now elderly, he was a small, thin man with thick wavy white hair. His controlled frenetic energy made him use his hands sparingly but emphatically. He had the coldness of the professional assassin paired with the calculating skill of a Finnish sniper.

Logan would prefer Herr Géza take a rolled-up

newspaper and beat him over the top of his head than deliver one of his famous blistering lectures.

"The prince of Bewachterberg will be attending the final concert this semester," the small man frigidly told him as he began his reprimand.

The fae magic permeating Bewachterberg made all languages understood no matter the native tongue of the speaker or listener. So while the maestro spoke in the tongue of his adopted country, Logan understood the words in English.

The sentences sounded like two stereo speakers, each broadcasting a separate language. The twining of languages was one of the disconcerting things Logan had experienced when arriving at Bewachterberg. Sometimes it gave him a headache and the dizzying feeling of being in two worlds at once. Today, Logan was too embarrassed to worry about his head hurting.

"Or does this matter with your loose American morals where everyone is equal despite ability?"

Logan mumbled an apology, bowing his head at his teacher's justified verbal assault.

"If you think as an exchange student you can, as you young people call it, blow this off and ditch rehearsal, you are very wrong, young man. Yes, music is art, and to do it well we must be inspired. But we must also work. Hard work. Without putting in the practice, you are no more an artist than someone who yells at the television, thinking they are a football coach."

Logan would have found the maestro's words funny if directed at anyone else. He couldn't imagine Herr Géza even owned a television or watched American football. Though maybe he meant soccer? Logan still hadn't figured all of that out yet.

To atone for his mistake, Logan got a long list of things to do in the practice room. Chairs needed to be folded and put away, music sheets sorted, and he was to hold himself ready for anything the concertmaster required him to do.

Late morning became the afternoon, and by the time he exited the building, the sun was starting to set. Realizing he still hadn't eaten all day, he dropped his violin off at the apartment and headed to a popular Biergarten located down the street.

The Weberhaus was once an 1800s textile factory, but through urban renewal, the derelict structure was renovated to a modern beer hall. The former factory building had several businesses carved out from its hollow interior. The Weberhaus Biergarten was a long and narrow rectangular section that went from the front to the back on the second floor. The interior was composed of wood, brick, and metal with industrial fans and tubing hanging from the ceiling, serving more as sculptural art than for any practical purpose.

Hanging on the distressed brick walls were colorful canvases displaying post-modern art. While the town's government wanted Geheimetür to continue looking like an 1890 oil painting, there was, in some circles, still a backlash against this aesthetic. While Bewachterberg had not been part of the 1989 art revolution that swept through Germany and the eastern countries, many fervently embraced modernistic art.

Popular with students, the place was usually noisy and filled with strangers. Logan didn't mind, just the opposite. The noise and bustle made him believe things were normal in his life.

The American entered through the front doors and received a blast of warm air, smelling of hops. He shouldered his way through the crowd to find a spot to sit.

The hardwood floors, scarred by decades of heavy machinery, were now home to tables and chairs, and long tables that seated groups. The Biergarten's communal tables encouraged people to meet strangers and leave as friends. It was a part of the atmosphere and culture that Logan usually enjoyed.

He picked a table, not recognizing anyone in the beer hall. The diners all exchanged nods but continued talking with their companions, deep in a conversation about Egyptian hieroglyphics.

Someone further down into the Biergarten shouted for a toast, "Ein prosit! Ein prosit!" before mounting the table and raising a glass high. Inevitably, the toast led to a sing-a-long with everyone in the Weberhaus joining in.

Part of Sibyl's magical allure was giving her lovers an intense enjoyment of life around them. The saturated sensation of emotions her Beguiling generated was heady and immensely addictive. Colors were so vibrant they almost smelled, while the taste and smell of food became virtually orgasmic.

When she left, all of that was gone. His life became nothing but dust and black and white. Things were drab, tasteless, and bland. Like a balloon filled to overcapacity - almost to the bursting point, now deflated, uncertain of his shape. Stretched past what he should have been, the removal of enjoying even the simplest of things sent him spiraling downward.

He felt like an addict in withdrawal.

For weeks after his breakup, Logan had little interest in food. As he dropped weight, becoming dangerously lethargic, he learned to push himself to eat. Eating, sleeping, and getting to class each day were small victories against Sibyl's Beguiling spell.

Upon the waiter's arrival, he ordered Bratkartoffeln, a dish of thinly sliced fried potatoes. He added some spicy sausage and asked for a bottle of their signature hot spicy German mustard.

No way would he let that witch win, he thought grimly.

Due to the crush, his food was slow to arrive. Waiting, Logan looked idly around the restaurant. A group of fae sitting at a table nearby drew his attention.

Until he had arrived at the university, he had never seen so many fae in his life. But here, in Bewachterberg where they sheltered, he found himself surrounded by a variety of clans, or Septs, as they preferred it.

He had made the mistake of thinking them just another form of humanity, but Sibyl had taught him the danger of giving human emotions and motivations to beings that were from another place. A dangerous lesson that, according to the fae nurse, would have a lasting consequence if he didn't figure out a way to escape Sibyl's Beguiling.

He guessed the group was some forest Sept for they were long stick-like creatures. While their faces were the bright green color of new leaves, their bodies were a dusky green-olive shade of brown with the texture of tree bark.

Their elongated triangular heads had alien, black almond-shaped eyes and slits for noses. Their arms and legs were held stiffly at 90-degree angles, reminiscent of tree branches.

The three creatures were leaning over the tabletop, talking in a confidential tone. Their mouths, round-like knotholes, made Logan think of goldfish mouths as they opened and closed.

He could feel that the fae group was about to commit some mischief involving a deception. He idly wondered who would be their victim. It sure wouldn't be him. He had enough dealings with the fae and their kind.

His order arrived, and Logan gave all his attention to food. He put a heavy dose of spicy mustard on top of everything, and he started eating with grim fortitude.

He was sipping his beer when he happened to see beverages delivered to the table of the forest fae. They got four mugs, and as the waiter left, they dropped something in the fourth one. At the action, the group shook with silent laughter.

That didn't seem fair.

Nothing made Logan angrier than foul play. It didn't sit well with his world view of truth and falsehood, black and white.

Before Logan could wonder more about their action, a black woman with her natural hair walked past him. She was short and slender, about his age, wearing a well-worn black leather jacket over a green t-shirt. She appeared human, but the pointed tips of her ears marked her as fae.

When she passed the table of the forest fae, the stick creatures excitedly bounced up in their seats, climbing over the counter before regaining their chairs. It seemed they were trying to convince her to sit with them. They must have convinced her, as she pulled over a chair.

One of them slid over the fourth beer, and in a flash, Logan knew what was about to happen.

"Don't drink it," said Logan. The three bog sprites stopped their chattering. "They put something in your drink."

The woman's hand which had been lifting the drink paused for a moment before returning the glass to the table.

"Sounds like something these leaf mites would do." The fae woman's voice held a slight accent, a hint of a dialect to her speech that Logan's musical ear noticed, yet couldn't identify. "I wondered about their sudden burst of friendliness."

The bog sprites, budded from the same tree root, had identical features. They chirped a quick denial to the human who had shoved his way into their business.

"What did you say?"

"What do you mean?"

"You talk nonsense, human."

The woman raised her eyebrows. "Are you accusing this human of lying?"

"Why does he come to our table?"

"You're not wanted, human."

"Fae and fae mind their own business."

Logan came from stubborn stock. He wasn't going to be intimidated by sticks from doing what was right.

"Then one of you drink it if it is so innocent?"

No one verbally responded to Logan's request, but the fae woman dipped a finger into the suspicious beer and brought it under her nose.

"Rowan Wattle and Mistletoe."

At her words, a trio of giggles burst out from her hyperactive companions. They climbed over the booth and table like unsupervised toddlers, disturbing stick monkeys.

"Flying high."

"Seeing visions."

"Back to faerie you'd go."

Logan noticed the fae woman didn't seem as amused. In a flash, she grabbed one of her companions by its neck and slammed the bog sprite down on the table. Beer glasses went flying across the slick table, shattering upon the floor.

Occupants further down the long table rescued their drinks and plates, getting up and moving away from the fae confrontation. The volume of the noisy crowd wound down to a few murmurs until the

Biergarten was silent. All eyes turned their way.

"Your little joke has cost you, twig," the fae woman snapped. Her fingers wrapped around the bog sprite's slender neck. "Under the Laws of Civility, I declare a Fiat of Harm. If you want to live, you can pay your Balance with the name of who put you up to this foolishness."

The other two bog sprites weren't strong enough to pull her off their companion. They nervously climbed up and down the table in agitated, repetitive pacing.

Despite being told never to interfere with fae matters, Logan started to feel sorry for the stick creature. He didn't feel wrong about intervening but was it right that the fae stick dies for an act never completed?

"No harm done, right? Maybe you could let him go?"

She looked up to give Logan an inscrutable, assessing stare from black eyes.

"For your intervention, we have a Debt but don't tell me how to Balance harm intended for me. That's not how Balance works."

She proceeded to shake the bog sprite's scrawny neck, making his triangular-shaped head bob like a toy. Her fingers squeezed harder until her fingertips met the heel of her palm.

"Your actions have put me in debt to this human." Her voice was hard with the threat. "Do you know how much I hate that idea?"

The bog sprite made a gurgling noise, unable to speak, while his companions hurriedly explained.

"No harm, just fun."

"Just a joke. A tease."

She replied in a flat tone, "Ha. Ha. I'm laughing so hard."

"She just wanted to teach you a lesson."

"Sibyl, the siren."

Given the name, the fae woman released her victim.

"See that wasn't so hard was it, you nasty little leaf mite."

Hopping off the table, the soles of her boots crushed the shards of glass to powder. "The Fiat of Harm I declared paid. *Expletus*."

Turning to Logan, she gave him a sharp nod of her head.

"C'mon human, where's your table?"

Logan led her back to his seat where a meaningful black-eyed glare and raised eyebrows made the person across from him suddenly vacate the area.

"Would you like something to eat?" he asked politely.

"I'll order it myself. I've already incurred enough of a debt to you."

"Oh, I don't mind."

"But I do," she responded curtly. She closed her eyes, digging the heels of her hands into their sockets, in a gesture that was tired or maybe frustrated. "The problem with humans is they don't understand how things work with us. I guess I'll have to explain it to you. You just saved my life back there."

"Let's not exaggerate."

She rolled her eyes, exasperated at his depreciating statement. She held up her hand to stop him from continuing.

"Let me finish, please. Rowan Wattle is a fungus toxic to humans, add mistletoe, and yeah that concoction wasn't innocent. A human would have died after drinking it. I guarantee I would, at the very least, have had a bad trip. Don't know if my sanity would have survived it."

She called over a waiter and gave her order, adding, "separate checks," before waving the man away and continuing with her explanation.

"We fae are pretty chaotic beings, but one thing we hold dear, and that is the Laws of Civility. I could deny you a Bond of Gratitude since you're human and humanity isn't our equals. But I keep the Balance even when others might put their finger to tip the scale. So just know I plan on fulfilling my Bond as quickly as possible."

"Does this mean you're my lifelong friend?" Logan asked, smiling. Surely she wasn't serious?

She grimaced in impatience.

"Fae relationships are about the connections of

mutual bonds, debts, favors, and yes, even contests of power define us. They help us understand who we can trust and what another will do in a tight spot."

By now the Biergarten had returned to its usual level of noise. The mess on the floor was quickly cleaned up. The three bog sprites were exiting out the front door but took time to spare a few shouted insults to the general ensemble which ignored them.

"I know Sibyl, who the leaf mites mentioned," Logan began again, feeling they had gotten off on the wrong foot. He added under his breath, "Unfortunately."

"What's your connection with that bird-brain?"

Logan gave a weak laugh. "Last semester, I thought I was in love."

"Oh."

"Pretty much."

"Frost on the pumpkin," cursed the woman and looked sideways, avoiding his gaze. "I guess getting you unhooked from that Beguiler's spell would pay off my Debt. Besides, that chickenpox, with her attempt at drugging me, committed a breach. I'll probably have to declare an open Fiat of Harm against her anyway."

Logan only heard the first part of what the woman said.

"Is that possible? I thought there was no way out of this curse? That's what Sibyl told me."

The fae woman was annoyed.

"Number one rule, don't believe anything a fae promises. The fae exists to make loopholes. Besides, I don't have much choice. Now that I've acknowledged the existence of a bond between us, I must pay it off to your satisfaction or suffer the consequences."

"Suffer? Why?"

"By the way, what's your name, human?"

"Logan Dannon."

For a moment, she seemed to hesitate before reaching her right hand over the table. Logan shook it. Her soft skin was a contradiction, both warm and cool.

"Brigit Cullen. I promise I'll have you out from under her spell before finals."

Chapter Five
Clean Sweep

Brigit arrived at Logan's apartment the next day carrying a bucket of cleaning supplies. With her was a fae she introduced as Granite.

"He's the muscle." Brigit used a thumb to indicate the bulky young man standing behind her who was holding a vacuum cleaner. "He's on the wrestling team."

Granite was big as a boulder, with a thick neck, and biceps that looked like basketballs. The wrestler gave a wave and greeted him, "Hey, human."

Retreating from the door he had opened to let them in, Logan carefully put away the violin he had been practicing on and latched down the case lid. Granite looked like the type of guy who'd think it hilarious to bounce a bow across the strings. And the wrestler's hands appeared powerful enough to crush the instrument's neck without trying.

Brigit placed her bucket on the kitchen counter and started opening up the cabinets, pulling out cleaning items such as sponges and spray bottles to join what she had brought.

"My apartment is pretty clean." Logan's protest elicited a laugh from Brigit and a deep chuckle from Granite who accented his humor by cracking his knuckles.

"We're here to do a deep clean, Logan," the fae woman said.

"Deep," repeated Granite, leaning his head left and right, giving his thick neck an audible popping noise.

"The first mistake you made, Logan," she continued, shaking an admonishing finger at him, "was letting Granite enter your home without questioning his intentions or laying ground rules on what he could do once he was inside. That's sloppy. Typical of humans. However, to take down a siren, you'll need to get on board with a new way of thinking."

Brigit walked past him, hands on hips, to survey his apartment. She had a smile on her face because she found deep satisfaction in getting things cleaned. It was a viewpoint she could never convince her former roommate to adopt.

"Always tackle the hardest area to clean first. It makes the rest of the job go quickly." She waved the others to follow her. In his bedroom, Brigit ushered Logan over to the bed where she commanded him to sit.

"Put your feet on the bed. You don't want them touching the floor. That could be dangerous."

"Dangerous?"

Brigit continued her lecture as if Logan hadn't spoken.

"We all have nasty nightmares, Logan. Don't think you're alone in that. Even fae have them. Like Boom-Boom here."

Granite scrunched his forehead, thinking. After a moment, he suggested tentatively, "Like a dream about not writing your mom her weekly letter?"

"That's a nightmare?" scoffed Logan.

"His mother is a harpy, Logan. I mean that literally, not figuratively, so yeah," explained Brigit, patting Granite on his broad shoulder.

Turning to Logan, she instructed him to lay back on the bed and close his eyes. He paused, looking between the two fae. He had just met them, but on the other hand he needed help. He leaned back.

"Just imagine your worst nightmare," explained Brigit. "We'll use your thoughts as bait."

His eyes popped open.

"Bait?"

"You've got a hardcore infestation in here, pal, and I'm not talking about cockroaches or mold. These nasty creatures are probably part of what is draining your energy. Fear, depression, sadness, it's like butter on toast to these monsters. You're as mouth-watering as a Thursday night buffet."

"That's the night they do prime rib," Granite helpfully explained, nodding sagely at Brigit's words.

Logan carefully considered the validity of Brigit's statement. Yes, he had vivid dreams since he was a child, but when Sibyl came into his life, they had intensified over time until they had become nightmares.

He spoke slowly, "I keep dreaming about a real event that happened on a vacation I spent in England. I was fourteen, and my family was visiting the country. When we were hiking in Wales, I got lost on that mountain, Snowdon, for several days."

Granite made a tremendous whack by banging the palms of his hands together, giving an explosive shout, "*Yr Wyddfa*?! Were you initiated on *Yr Wyddfa*? By Earth and Air, Brigit you've caught yourself a live one here."

At the woman's puzzled look, Granite grew gleeful.

"He's a bard, Brig. He spent a night on the mountain considered to be Merlin's seat in the

Perilous Realm. You become a true bard when you survive the trials. Snowdon makes some of the greatest - like Taliesin. Don't you know your human history?"

She gasped and jumped back from Logan as if she just learned he had a contagious disease.

"A bard? You didn't tell me."

Logan licked his lips nervously. While women loved the sweet talk his silver-tongue could produce, when they discovered he could discern lies from truth, things usually soured.

Discovering he was a bard, Sibyl had toyed with his talent. She would feed him half-truths, trying to learn his limits.

Logan wondered how it would affect his budding relationship with Brigit.

Apparently, it just frustrated the dryad. She cried out, waving her fists in the air, as she stormed back and forth in quick pacing. "All these coincidences. What did I do to deserve this? Is there some goddess working against me?"

Logan mumbled, "could be," but Brigit didn't seem to hear his comment, as she was too busy lamenting her fate.

"Could this situation get any more complicated for me?"

Strangely, the dryad's turmoil made Logan feel more comfortable with her. Brigit's emotions were raw and real, unlike Sibyl's. His ex had never been upset by anything Logan did. Only in hindsight did he realize her calm acceptance of his quirks meant she had never cared.

Brigit shook out her hands and arms as if physically removing her aggravation.

"Okay, first things first. Let's begin with that dream. Lay down again, put your head on the pillows. Close your eyes, and tell me about how the nightmare starts."

Logan returned to his former position and, lacing his hands over his flat stomach, began again.

"We are climbing up, and I'm the last one in line. I don't notice I was falling behind my father's steps until I was alone. Surrounded by mist. Foggy. Now, I can't see anything. Without the sun, moon, or stars, it's impossible to know which direction to go. I keep shouting the names of my family. I even use my grandmother's real name. But no one answers."

Logan felt his palms grow sweaty as Brigit whispered close to his ear, "Keep going." The dryad had carefully climbed onto the mattress and was now lying beside him.

"I start hearing noises. It sounds like a scuffling sound from an animal in the brush. I get the feeling something is after me, following me. It's watching me. I can't see it. I'm sure something is stalking me."

Before Logan could continue further, Brigit

suddenly bounced up to her feet. Jumping up and down in excitement on the mattress, she shouted, "Boom-Boom, don't let it get away!"

Logan snapped open his eyes to see Granite wrestling with a waking nightmare.

About the size of a Rottweiler, the monster had a long segmented body with a chitin exoskeleton that glowed green. Its claw snapped dangerously close to Granite's head as the fae furiously grappled with its writhing body. The creature hissed furiously and the wrestler responded by tightening his stranglehold around its thorax.

Brigit grabbed the blanket folded at the end of his bed and handed Logan a corner.

"Let's throw this over the tail stinger."

Logan, still shocked at the appearance of such a creature, hastily complied with her suggestion. Thankfully, their aim was good. It landed over the creature's body and covered not only the stinger but its single eyestalk.

The fae wrestler quickly changed his position, rolling the creature in the blanket like a burrito to contain the monster. Granite's fists rained down hammer blows on the thrashing thing. Under their relentless ferocity, the monster's movements grew slower and slower. Ultimately, it became still, and the sticky syrup seeping into the carpet told the story's ending.

"It was under your bed," Brigit explained helpfully.

In one bound, she jumped off the mattress onto the floor, avoiding the carcass.

"I...how... Sibyl put that there?" he finally asked, incredulous. Logan rubbed a hand over his forehead. His fingers ruffled his hair, so it stuck up sideways in a lopsided wave.

"It was a tulpa. Without protective boundaries set, it probably was spawned by your own fears."

Granite added, "A nice size, too! Brigit said I'd have a workout. Thanks, human."

Brigit continued explaining, "Tulpas feed off the emotions of their creator, until they eventually become self-aware. Luckily for you, Logan, you have me as your personal pest exterminator."

Instead of giving Brigit any credit, Logan looked at Granite who was taking off his syrup soaked t-shirt exposing a well defined six pack.

"Thank you. Are you okay?"

The fae wrestler returned Logan's concern with a sideways smirk.

"Never better. Brigit promised that I could take the body with me. That's not a problem, is it?"

"No," replied Logan, rather loudly.

"Good! It's going to make the coolest beer stein. The guys in the house are going to be so jealous."

Brigit cleared her throat, gaining their attention. She indicated the closet with a toss of her head and started speaking in an unnaturally loud voice.

"Now, if some monsters can be reasonable, perhaps their body won't become a beer stein or a rug."

The closet door, which had been slowly opening during the battle, now opened all the way. From the darkness stepped forward a domed hairy haystack of a creature, a thousand tiny eyestalks emerging from its coarse coat of black fur. Its many eyestalks waved frantically about in opposite directions, giving it a harried, panicked air. It stood on two long chicken feet.

Its shrieking voice was as piercing and irritating as nails down a chalkboard.

"If I'm no longer needed, I shall go."

But the closet monster's attempt at dignity was interrupted by a jeer from Brigit.

"Never needed and never wanted. Boom-Boom, escort it from the premises."

"No need to rush me," said the monster loftily, which earned it a knock on its head from Granite as the wrestler said, "Do you want more of Boom-Boom?"

The creature remained silent and scurried from the room on its chicken feet. Granite followed it, shouting back he'd return later to collect his winnings.

Hearing the front door close, Logan collapsed onto the mattress. Brigit looked down at him, pleased.

"Yes, Logan, you need someone like me around here. I'll stay right here, take that extra bedroom, and pay off my favor to you. Like a bodyguard. You'll never know that I'm here. I'll be quiet as a mouse."

Chapter Six
Moving Day

By removing the sigil, the memory of having an extra bedroom returned to Logan, and without any further adieu, Brigit claimed it.

The dryad figured it didn't really matter that she had moved in a week before Granite's removal of the tulpa monsters. It would probably upset the human if he knew, so she avoided revealing the entire truth.

Brigit justified the subterfuge because she was helping him.

Still, ridding him of the creatures living in his bedroom did not, in her estimation, repay the total amount of her debt. Brigit owed him a Bond.

Besides, Logan was intimately tied in a Fiat of

Harm with Brigit's enemy, making them both united against a common threat.

Considering what Sibyl revealed during her recent visit to Brigit's workplace, it appeared the siren had a possessive streak. The dryad guessed her use of Logan's spare room pushed Sibyl to retaliate through the bog sprites.

By the Laws of Civility, Brigit could justify killing Sibyl as part of maintaining Balance. At the very least, Brigit would soon need to publicly announce a Fiat against Sibyl. If she did not, the dryad would lose status amongst her community at the college.

Sibyl though was much higher in the Fae's natural hierarchy than bog sprites. Killing or harming her would result in possible repercussions from her bondmates, a situation that could hoist Brigit into a complicated fae vendetta of Challenges and Bonds.

Brigit had kept a low profile at the university, making sure her debts were small. Now, incurring a Debt of Gratitude and a Fiat of Harm in one day irked Brigit.

Brigit decided to make today her official move-in day. Before leaving for her own classes, the wood sprite emptied her backpack. She sorted out her books and returned her biology lab book, a notepad, and some pens and pencils back into its interior. When she hitched the bag over her shoulder, it felt ridiculously light now.

She locked the front door and bent down to talk with the coco mat. Ownership wasn't a concept it clearly understood. The dryad cautioned it not to discuss any of their business and not to commit behavior allowing entrance.

You're not to let anyone know we're at home. That's for the door and its peephole, Brigit explained yet again.

Welcome! Wipe feet! Wait to welcome?

Exactly, agreed Brigit. She promised it a proper cleaning and brushing when she returned. Turning to the plant, she showed it some mental pictures of different planters available at work. After it told her its preference, Brigit said goodbye and headed to the stairwell.

At the corner, she found a town trolley. Flashing her student ID, she got a ride to the main campus. Maybe she'd look for a bike now that she had an apartment where she could store it.

It was a quirky town with the archaic next to the latest tech. The country of Bewachterberg was restrictive about traffic: personal vehicles could not enter Old Geheimetür, and only electric-powered cars were allowed on the city outskirts. So it wasn't unusual to see electrically-powered trolleys and delivery vans pass horses pulling wagons.

Due to its growth in the last four decades, the university's more recent construction was nestled throughout the city, surrounded by older venerable buildings. However, the original campus remained almost untouched. Walking across the green, if Brigit ignored the students in modern clothes, she could imagine what it was like hundreds of years back.

The original buildings were once a monastery. In 1521, the holy brothers had been removed and replaced with Protestants under the order of Bewachterberg's king. It eventually became a place of learning.

What was once the abbey and cloister now housed the library, the monk's frater had become space for administration offices, and the infirmary was one of several cafeterias spread across the campus grounds.

Hearing the bells of the tower ringing to mark the noon hour, Brigit quickened her steps to visit the mother oak. When she reached the tree, the wood sprite impulsively wrapped her skinny arms about its trunk. Its circumference was so large her hands couldn't touch. Laying her cheek against its bark, she felt the power of its wisdom and strength vibrate under her skin.

"Thanks, revered one, for looking after me. I'll be taking my things today but don't worry. I'll stop by every day to talk with you, my first and best friend."

The oak's canopy whispered with its leaves, and it rained down some of last season's acorns. A few nuts fell on top of Brigit's hair, causing her to grin.

"Good idea," she said as she bent down to collect the oak's offering.

She examined each of them for quality and kept only those that still had their acorn cap intact and had no insect holes or water damage. Finding four good handfuls that met her criteria, the fae woman carefully stuck them into the outer pocket of her backpack.

Standing up, she placed her hand on the oak's bark and opened a passage into the Perilous Realm. Stepping lightly across the magical threshold, she entered the interior of the tree and into the realm of the Perilous.

The area was not infinite in size; it was about the dimensions of a small room, but one filled with soft golden light. Brigit surveyed the work needing to get done before she'd have to run across campus to make her lab class.

Her goal of getting everything packed up wouldn't happen if she just stood there. Unzipping her backpack, she got started.

Picking up her clothes one by one, she took each item between her hands, folding them smaller and smaller, tighter and tighter, until they were almost as small as the nail on her pinkie finger.

Making big things tiny was a fae art form universal

to all the Septs.

She popped off the cap of one of the acorns and tapped the top of the nut with a forefinger, creating a pocket of the Perilous within it. This act of magic provided Brigit plenty of room within the acorn to pack her clothes.

Once her acorn suitcase was stuffed, the dryad closed the top of the nut with a bit of spit. The liquid also served as a glue to keep the replaced acorn cap securely on top. Brigit placed the first acorn suitcase in a pocket of her backpack separate from her books. She repeated the process with the other acorns until all her clothes and personal items were stored.

Done, she zipped her bag closed, pulling her arms through the backpack's shoulder straps. She opened the doorway back to the human lands and jumped through only to bump into Celia who was leaning against the oak waiting for her.

"I thought I'd find you here," her bondmate said, steadying Brigit with a hand on the fae's upper arm.

The naiad was one of the few fae Brigit allowed this close to her. Since they were both naturals, one naiad, one dryad, they had felt an immediate kinship upon meeting last semester. Celia's family was of a healing variety, and there was no way the nurse-in-training would harm someone unless it were a matter of life or death.

No foolish Challenges for Celia's kind.

"Let's walk and talk," said Brigit, "as we are tight on time."

The two young women fell into a quick step, almost a jog, beside each other. They would need to hurry to make their class on the opposite end of the campus grounds.

Celia was a bit taller than Brigit, and her chestnut curls, wrapped in a colorful headscarf, bounced behind her as they trekked across the quad.

"I heard about what happened last night at Weberhaus."

"Hm," was Brigit's only reply. Fae loved to gossip, but they often got the details wrong. It was best to wait and hear what Celia thought she knew.

"How could you have gotten into a Debt of Gratitude with a human? You weren't supposed to go so far."

"Huh?!" Brigit stuttered in surprise. "You admit an ulterior motive suggesting Logan's apartment to me?"

"Yes. But I'm a healer, Brigit. When he showed up at student health services, I couldn't leave the guy to die because Sibyl needed another conquest."

At Celia's injured tone, Brigit apologized. Her companion was a kindhearted naiad. There was no way Celia could have ignored a wounded puppy. It took a siren, with a predatory heart to devour a human innocent.

"Why did you think I could help?"

"You know everyone. And most of the fae at LOTTOS like you. Even when you incur a Debt, you make it small, so it doesn't overwhelm the one who owes it."

Brigit felt exposed by Celia's observation as it was startlingly close to a plan she wasn't ready to explain. It was smarter to keep things on the quiet when it came to schemes. Even with beings you liked.

"And you're clever."

Brigit flashed a smile at the compliment. "Thanks."

"And Sibyl isn't."

"Sibyl may not be a brain surgeon, but she's good at being a Beguiler," cautioned Brigit. "Getting her to unhook a human isn't going to be easy."

"I don't know why her court allowed her to come here in the first place if she can't control her baser fae desires. Now, there's a ridiculous rumor she's aiming her sight even higher. As high as the prince of Bewachterberg."

"That guy? I thought Sibyl was dating that polo team guy, whats-his-face?"

The two had arrived at the science hall, and Celia held open the door for Brigit, following behind.

"She is. And the polo team lost their match last week since the captain is now obsessed with her."

"Yeah, being drained by a Beguiler can really throw you off your game," said Brigit. Celia wasn't done and interrupted her. "The administration is talking about restricting fae enrollment despite the Treaty of Sigismund."

Brigit growled at Celia's remark. "Sibyl doesn't seem to see the big picture. It's actions like hers which will get us banned from Bewachterberg. No other human college will let us enroll, let alone let us live openly amongst them."

"Tell me about it!" exclaimed Celia. "I've got one more year to go. If Sibyl capsizes the boat, I'm without a degree."

Unlike Brigit's own parents, Celia's family encouraged her to pursue a degree at Leopold-Ottos-Universität. They hoped that by combining Western medicine with fae healing, it would increase the public appeal of their spa services.

Celia continued her rant, exhibiting a rare bitterness.

"Sibyl doesn't care. She only came here to find a hapless human with money and social standing to make herself famous. She's out of here as soon as she finds a better meal ticket, leaving who knows what devastation behind her when she runs off with her prince."

Behind lab goggles, Celia used pipettes to mix chemicals while Brigit recorded the results. They continued talking over their problem, and so Brigit learned another interesting tidbit of gossip: the brownie caring for Sam had left his apartment.

"Last weekend, they had a huge scene. Pots and pans were flying. The ruckus was so loud that the neighbors called the Geheimetür police. The brownie accused Sam of making her into a boggart because of his filthy ways. She said she was done with him forever."

"Rotten peaches!" Brigit exclaimed in astonishment.

During her time as Sam's roommate, she had known the brownie had been unhappy. It was that unhappiness Brigit had hoped to exploit to win the hob to the dryad's cause.

"From the sound of that fight are you sure she hasn't turned into a boggart already? To treat a hob poorly causes them to change pretty quickly."

"I don't think she is yet. Just mad and feeling used. She made the police write a report about not having a day off since arriving. She accused Sam of domestic slavery. The authorities asked her to stay until they decided if charges are filed."

With a sly smile, Celia added, "Didn't she always like you?"

Chapter Seven
Pony Express

rownies were of the fae Sept called the Kindly Ones. Unlike most of the other fae clans, they liked to be around humans, taking care of the mundane tasks around the house and farm.

Being very dedicated to cleaning, brownies didn't like to talk while they worked. They didn't care to be spied upon or judged by the householder. Mistreating a brownie could cause them to leave without warning, or, if they felt abused, could transform them into a darker being.

What humans called poltergeists were often brùnaidh evolved into malicious boggarts.

However, while hobs were touchy, they weren't as solitary as all the stories made them out to be. Before Brigit left Sam's apartment so abruptly, she had enjoyed several long and friendly conversations with the brùnaidh.

Still, Brigit knew to contact the brownie without offending her would be a task requiring subtlety. You could not ask a Kindly One directly for aid. They did not like being bidden to do anything, being notoriously proud and easily offended.

Nonetheless, there was something to be said about growing up in a royal faerie court. The stifling etiquette and the diplomatic dance had given Brigit skills.

The brownie was a challenge, but the dryad had some ideas.

After grabbing a quick dinner with Celia, Brigit studied in the library until nightfall. Once the stars started to emerge, she left and crossed the quad. Along the way, she patted the great mother oak, before continuing her walk to the very edge of the main campus.

This park area ended at a newer road and sidewalk that took students to several apartment complexes. However, Brigit turned left, adopting an older footpath. Here she left the manicured lawns behind to enter a wild woodland.

The dirt track was once a well-traveled cut-through to the main campus, but it was now obsolete due to the new roadway. Losing this route was not considered a significant loss for the human students, for the old footpath made many afraid.

Even during daylight hours, the thick tree canopy cast the area with shadows. However, it was the eerie feeling of being watched, that caused humans to run the entire length of the trail, finding themselves breathless and shaking when they emerged into the light.

Being fae, Brigit knew exactly what watched.

At the halfway point, the path crossed a stone bridge, at least a hundred years old. This bridge transversed a small creek, far deeper than it initially appeared and flowing slowly for it was a tributary to the wide river that bisected Old Geheimetür.

The dryad crossed halfway before giving a low whistle of three notes, sending out a call.

The fae used several messaging services. The first and easiest was birds. However, using winged messengers could possibly play into the siren's hands.

Another possibility was using trees. They passed the news from root to root, or when the wind blew just right, from leaf to leaf. While this would have been the dryad's natural choice, it was slow, and they couldn't transport packages.

So she would need someone who could use water to bring her a package.

Water, more than any of the seven elements the fae recognized, served as the perfect portal for traveling. Water did not have individuality like stone or wood. One drop, placed with others, merged seamlessly. Compounded with water's ability to flow, it made it a perfect conductor.

However, using water was a method best left to those with that affiliation. As all water was one, finding direction within the fairy waterways could be tricky, if not impossible.

You could become lost in the murky depths or worse, drown, crossing the Perilous using fairy waterways.

It didn't take long before Brigit could see some dark mass moving under the water, traveling towards her. The the head of a black horse broke the water's surface. Silently, gliding closer it caused few ripples in the water, as more of its body appeared.

It was a kelpie, a water-horse, and a Beguiler.

She pulled back from the edge of the parapet, careful to keep a safe distance as the being approached. This kelpie had sworn off enticing people to climb on its back to drown them, but Brigit knew promises among the fae could be easily forgotten.

Under the dimness of the crescent moon, the being's equine shape faded as the kelpie assumed a human form. Like most shapeshifters, his body was in superb physical condition, and his appearance might explain why he was such a favored courier.

The water was now at his hips. He moved his hands back and forth in the water, causing small waves. The liquid splashed upon his chest where droplets sparkled over his smooth skin. He had a long black braid of hair, thick as a horse's tail, hanging down between his shoulder blades.

"What could I do for a young wood sprite this evening?"

Eying his broad shoulders and muscled chest, Brigit could think of several things but since they weren't about the brownie she didn't mention them.

"I'd like to request a package purchase and delivery."

This kelpie made a lucrative living as a mail carrier since the fae students in Geheimetür were homesick for packages and news from the Perilous Realm.

"Where?"

"Islay, the Inner Hebrides."

"Och Aye. It be me native waters, but I think ye knows that Brigit Cullen. I think ye know it might be a favorite of a certain hob too. A cleaning acquaintance who recently liberated herself from a

Bond of Servitude."

She returned his smile. He was of the same court as the brùnaidh. Brigit was glad that her guess that the brownie had shared her woes with him was proved correct.

"What do ye want from Islay?" he asked. His voice was deep and as seductive as water for those in a desert.

"A bottle of fine Scotch whiskey," said the dryad, naming a distillery.

"Would that be a gift for a certain someone?"

While Beguilers generally couldn't be-spell their fellow fae, it didn't stop him from being damned attractive in his own right. He walked closer to the bridge, his hips moving in a mesmerizing manner.

"Perhaps," said Brigit, trying not to be persuaded from the topic. "But what's the fee?"

The kelpie gave her a choice on payment, favors to be determined or coinage accepted in the human lands. Brigit told him, "I'm surprised you take the human money, but yes, that is how I prefer to pay."

Before the dryad could reach into her pocket, the kelpie cupped his hands and threw a wave of water up over the side of the bridge. The spray hit her in the face, and Brigit involuntarily blinked.

The dryad opened her eyes to find the kelpie far too close. When she jumped back, her butt hit the stone bridge. She was trapped between his arms and chest. He bent down, dripping water over her as he said, "Dinnae be so shy, sprite."

"I'm not shy," stuttered Brigit, filled with equal amounts of desire and terror. She had no affinity for water, and if he grabbed her, the trees were too far away to help her. The other problem was his wet nakedness made the kelpie's masculinity very apparent.

His mouth was close to her ear as he whispered, "I've heard ye've run afoul of our blond beauty. Dinnae ye think ye could use a bondmate?"

Brigit gulped but shook her head no, not trusting her voice. He gave a laughing neigh and backed off, finding a spot to sit cross-legged on the parapet's wall.

"It be too easy to tease ye, wood sprite."

Wanting to change the subject, she brought Logan's wallet from the back pocket of her jeans. She didn't feel guilty about taking it for if her plan succeeded, it would benefit Logan.

Besides, she was trying to teach him to be more careful of his person and possessions. If tough love was required, Brigit was more than capable of dispensing it.

"Why did you have to scare me? I just wanted to sacrifice a dram at Walensee in memory of the old brownie."

Brigit grew up with a mother who could fake tears in a heartbeat. Taught by a master, she whipped up some moisture, touching the wet corners of her eyes with her forefinger. The kelpie smirked, giving a slow clap in appreciation.

"Well played, dryad. But the brùnaidh says she's done with all ye lazy slobs. I dinnae think ye be persuading the Broonie."

"Oh, I perfectly understand why she's fed up. Remember, I also lived with Sam."

"Aye right. I willnae be telling ye yer business. If ye pay the fare, I'll dae the pickup."

Lake Walen in Switzerland lay outside the borders of Bewachterberg. It was an area Brigit had often heard the brownie compare to her home lochs of Scotland.

It would be an excellent place to implement the dryad's plan.

She took a bus as far she could, and than used portals of the Perilous Realm to continue her journey. Brigit skipped fast through the portals, not wanting to be tracked or accosted by any other fae.

The dryad eventually stepped out of boulder in a picturesque but desolate area surrounding the lake.

Granite had recommended choosing a spot on the Churfirsten mountain range because the cliffs would ensure few tourists. Brigit was glad she brought her jacket as the altitude made it quite chilly even though it was late spring. Looking up, she could see snow on the peaks.

It was high up, a place that you might find goats but not many humans. Far, far below was the lake, its green-blue water winking diamonds under the noonday sun.

It made the perfect place to enjoy a song and dram, hopefully with company.

Brigit wedged her back against the hard cliff face and unpacked her backpack, setting up a picnic. In a handmade ceramic bowl, she poured a rich cream. It was an organic brand, and the box said the cows were grass-fed. That sounded old-fashioned enough to appeal to a brùnaidh. Come to think of it, Brigit didn't know what cows would eat other than grass.

She had picked up the bottle of whiskey from the kelpie the night before. When she casually mentioned she would be at Churfirsten the next day, he had given her a wink and a nod before vanishing back into the depths of his stream.

Brigit set the bottle on the grass, alongside two glasses and a plate. The dryad broke the seal on the whiskey and took a whiff of its contents.

Gosh! That was potent!

Making sure the two glasses were secure on the ground, she poured some into both. One glass she put near her hand, but the other she set down on a flat-topped rock just out of her reasonable reach.

From a brown paper bag, she pulled out two scones

bought that very morning from her favorite bakery. She set them on the plate and put that beside the second glass.

Next, Brigit pulled out a sandwich and ate her lunch while enjoying the scenery. When she finished, she dusted off the crumbs before beginning a ritual she hoped would tempt the hob to visit.

Brigit started singing, softly at first, letting her throat feel the music. Her song built in volume until it was quite loud, floating away with the wind that was chapping her cheeks.

She hoped the hob didn't mind if it was a bit out of key. It was the intent that mattered, right?

"*Should auld acquaintance be forgot, and never brought to mind? Should auld acquaintance be forgot, and auld lang syne?*"

Brigit went through the entire verse, and by the second round, she heard a faint sound behind her. Smiling slightly, she took up the song again, this time the dryad's words were repeated in a thick Scottish brogue.

"*Shid ald akwentans bee firgot, an nivir brocht ti mynd? Shid ald akwentans bee firgot, an ald lang syn?*"

They continued singing, their voices gaining enthusiasm as they reached the last chorus together.

"*And there's a hand my trusty friend! And give me a hand o' thine! And we'll take a right good-will draught, for auld lang syne.*"

Brigit picked up her glass and took a swig, causing her to quickly suck in air to prevent a cough.

When there was nothing but silence, Brigit reached for the spare glass and was about to turn it over to allow the liquid to soak the earth. A loud voice blasted into her ear.

"Dinnae ye be pouring good Scotch whiskey to the ground, Brigit Cullen! That be a waste of pure gold."

Brigit stopped her hand and returned the glass on its rock.

"I was only going to give an offering to the spirits of this place for this beautiful view."

She sipped more slowly the second time. Looking over the lake, she could see from the corner of her eyes a hairy brown hand pick up the glass and snatch one of the scones.

"It's a bonnie spot," Brigit repeated.

"Och aye," the brùnaidh agreed, but the being did not expand on her comment.

There was the contented smacking of the brownie's lips as she enjoyed her repast. It took another refill of the glass before the being spoke again.

"I hear ye be on the dark side of that screwball siren, lassie."

"She's upset that I'm rooming with a former beau of hers."

"The siren's a possessive bit, fae-feral she is. Dinnae know why she be at such a place as LOTTOS."

"What's stupid about it," fumed Brigit, wanting a sympathetic ear to vent to, "is we are just roommates. Nothing romantic about it. So I'm not taking any of this guy's heart space. But now she's forced me into a corner about defending him. And he's human to boot."

"Be careful. She be wicked, even for fae. Mean-spirited."

This time the brownie poured for them both while saying, "Though, I'd lay a handful down on the table that she dinnae know what tiger's tail she grabbed."

"She's about to learn," said Brigit darkly.

The hob took up the bowl of cream and started sipping from it. It left a bit of a milk mustache on her hairy upper lip, but Brigit was careful not say anything about it. You did not win a Kindly One over by commenting on their appearance.

"You might know the human she's Beguiled. By the last name, he's a countryman of yours. He goes by Logan Dannon."

At the sound of it, the hob's hand paused before slowly bringing the bowl back to her lips for another sip. Brigit waited patiently to see what the hob would say.

The brownie took her time, finally putting down the bowl and wiping her face with the back of her hairy hand before saying, "I recognize it."

Brigit raised her eyebrows.

"Illustrious is it?"

The brùnaidh cackled like a crone and jumped lightly to her big feet. Her height brought her as tall as Brigit's knee.

"I know what ye be wanting, lassie, so I'll be putting you on probation. Ye and the laddie. But understand this, I can and will leave when I want. When I want to go, I'll go. No explanation."

To show agreement with the terms, Brigit silently held out the bottle. With a snatch and grab, the brownie took it before disappearing into the earth.

Chapter Eight
Setting Boundaries

ach morning Logan found Brigit in his kitchen. Oddly, he found her presence comforting. Like she was a lucky charm or protection against others of her kind.

This morning, she had fixed breakfast: a stack of blueberry pancakes, which sounded delicious after a good night's sleep without monsters feasting on his dreams.

"Oh, this isn't due to me," she said, taking no credit for the feast. "We have a brownie now."

"What's a brownie?"

"It's a house fae, one of the Kindly Ones because they enjoy being around humans and helping them.

She's going to be a great asset, but there are rules which you need to know."

Before she outlined the rules, the fae woman changed subjects, "By the way, don't leave your wallet on the counter. It's not safe."

Logan caught the folded wallet she tossed to him. While he was tucking it safely into his back pocket, Brigit swiftly gave him a hard pinch on his arm.

"Ow! Why did you do that?"

"Boundaries, Logan, boundaries." Brigit quickly retreated so he couldn't return the favor. She leaned her butt against the counter rim and continued her lecture. "You can't let a fae within arm's reach of you. That pinch was mild considering what one of us might do to you."

Logan took a seat at the breakfast table, carefully scooting his chair out of her reach. He sliced his pancakes into bite-size squares and poured syrup over them. He was about to put the fork into his mouth when he stopped.

"You didn't poison this, did you?" he asked her suspiciously.

"You're learning!" Brigit gave him two thumbs up but agreed they were not poisoned or tainted in any way. While he ate, she tidied up the kitchen. She rinsed off her plate and silverware, stacking them on the drainboard to the left of the sink while she explained the rules of having a brownie.

"She'll cook and clean for us, but she'll only stay if you abide by the rules."

"And those are?" Logan asked around a delicious mouthful. After one bite of his breakfast, he realized he needed a brownie.

"She works when you sleep. Don't stay up to try to sneak a peek of her. That's rude."

"Like Santa Claus?"

"Each night, leave a gift for her by the stove. The stove represents the hearth of the home since we don't have a fireplace here."

"Like a tip?"

"Exactly. Like a bowl of cream, milk, or porridge. The brùnaidh is also partial to cake and whiskey." Brigit continuing explaining about their new helper.

"Don't comment about what she does. I know your human impulse will be to praise or complain about her work but never say it out loud. She'll leave us or worse, become a boggart."

"A boggart?"

"Not a being we want around here. Those types do malicious mischief."

Logan was surprised to see his plate was clean of food. It was the first time in months he had felt hungry. He cleared his throat by drinking some of the milk in the glass beside his plate.

"I guess I don't understand how these favors, gifts, and things work? It sounds complicated. I'm bound to take a wrong step."

Brigit crossed her arms and tried to explain it all over again. Surely Logan was smarter than a coco mat?

"The fae don't do things for nothing. Unlike humans, every action we do for, or against, another being has to be Balanced. If you help someone study for a test, they, in turn, should bring you a housewarming gift."

"Naturally," Logan nodded his head. "That's just manners."

"You say that but how many times have you helped someone and got nothing in return?"

"It happens. Some people are selfish or rude. But giving can be its own reward."

Brigit looked at him as if Logan had gone insane.

"That's not how we think," she said, slowly shaking her head in the negative. "We form connections due to obligations owed between us. Who we form a debt with, as well as how we pay it, elevates or destroys our reputation. I admit that some fae believe maintaining Balance and the Laws of Civility are old-fashioned models, but it's a system that works."

"Like a code of chivalry?"

"That's a pretty good analogy, if you must use human terms. But always remember we are cutthroat. Without a system, we would fall into anarchy." Reflecting on her experiences, Brigit added, "The entire PR delights in playing with chaos regularly so maybe anarchy is desired by some."

"PR?"

"Perilous Realm."

When Logan got up to clean his plate, he waited for Brigit to move away from the sink before moving in to wash his dish.

"For instance," she continued, "when you told me about that poisoned brew at Weberhaus, I could have refused to acknowledge a debt between us simply because you're human. However, by conceding a Debt of Gratitude exists between us, it reflects well upon us both. For you, it increases your standing among the fae because I've elevated you to a fae being's level. Got it?"

"Kinda. But how does the debt thing work? How do you know how much you owe or when your tab is paid off? Who keeps the score?"

"You should have spoken up at the Biergarten once I said that I owed you. As the holder of the debt, it's up to you to outline the rules. But since you weren't aware this, I set the rules myself."

"Mighty decent of you."

Logan's grin got an answering smile from Brigit.

"For the future, though, know that when a Debt of Gratitude is announced, you need to step forward and claim it. Make at least three criteria. First, outline the task that must be done to complete the Balance.

Second, always stipulate that the fae can't harm you or yours during the finishing of the task. And last, provide a time frame."

"So what about our Gratitude bond? What are the boundaries?"

"First, the task is getting your heart free from Sibyl's claws."

"I thought getting rid of those monsters in my bedroom paid off the debt? That seemed like a pretty big favor to me."

"Not good enough for me." Brigit did not explain to him that saving her from being killed meant a bigger payback than vanquishing a couple of tulpas.

"Besides, Sibyl tried to harm me the other night so not only do I have a Debt bond with you, but I also have a Challenge, a Fiat of Harm, to settle with her. Saving you would kill two birds with one stone."

Logan knew how tricky the fae could be, but since Brigit seemed forthcoming, he tentatively asked, "You could just let me die. Wouldn't that absolve you of this debt thing?"

"Yes, but not in an honorable way." At Logan's look of relief, Brigit cautioned him, "Hey, I'm not saying fae haven't used that method before, but only a low-ranking being would stoop to such. Like those bog sprites. But not a dryad like me."

She picked up an apple from the bowl on the table and paused, holding it high and rotating it before her eyes to examine it.

"Of course, the simplest method would be to kill her."

"I don't want her dead," Logan cried out in alarm.

"Good. I'm glad you've got some common sense as I wasn't sure if you were the bloodthirsty type. Killing Sibyl would indeed be the simplest and fastest solution. Since she attempted harm against me, I would be justified within the Laws of Civility to repay her in this manner. But in the long run, it would result in all sorts of problems with her bondmates retaliating in kind."

"Like a vendetta? Such as Romeo and Juliet?" Logan asked, receiving a nod of affirmation from the dryad.

Brigit bit into the apple and continued talking with her mouth full. "Meanwhile, let's get your defenses in place. Once she realizes we have a Debt of Gratitude, she'll come after us both pretty hard. Best be ready. When is your first class today?"

"I have to make up some time by helping at the practice hall today. If I don't get there by one, my head will be on the chopping block."

"Okay. That gives you time to stop by the studio."

"Studio?" Logan raised an eyebrow. Brigit gave him a thumbs up for asking another question before handing him a business card.

"The simplest defense against the fae is iron.

Generally, we can't stand the stuff. There's an artist in the town square. She makes jewelry, Goth stuff, out of iron. That should do in a pinch. Pick out something you can wear every day. Bracelets, rings, something like that."

"Are you sure I can do that by myself?"

"Not really. But iron gives me the willies so I can't help you."

Keeping in mind what Brigit had told him about boundaries, Logan made her swear many binding things: she could not touch his violin, could not damage or remove anything from the apartment, and could not enter his bedroom or bathroom without his presence.

At each of his demands, she smiled, nodding her head, agreeing with his requests. By the end of his recital, she was openly laughing but not in derision.

"You're a fast learner, Bard. You might get out of this in one piece after all."

When Logan exited the auditorium hall, he found Brigit under a tree waiting for him.

"Lay down in the grass," she commanded without opening her eyes.

He did as she requested, but made sure he was more than an arm's length away from the dryad for

Logan hadn't forgotten their morning conversation.

If Brigit's lessons got him released from Sibyl's spell, he would do anything she asked. But, she didn't need to know that.

"Do you feel it?"

"What?"

"The energy?" He closed his eyes and tried, but couldn't sense it. "I love that about the human lands. So much vibration and power. Not like back home."

Logan suspected asking about the PR wasn't a good idea, so he said nothing. Brigit could make conversation for two.

"We need to announce a Fiat against Sibyl."

He wondered if Brigit said things like this to startle humans, so he decided to wait for an explanation. The dryad rolled over to her side, propping up her head with a bent elbow, and under her penetrating stare, Logan said, "Sounds dangerous to me."

"Of course it is."

"A Fiat is a fight, right? How would I stand a chance at winning a duel with a fae? I don't know anything about pistols, swords or magic. I'm not a wizard."

"Using swords in a duel to mark the forehead is human stuff. We don't do those types of showdowns. Well, not many of us would," conceded Brigit, who was trying to be as truthful as possible with this human. She rolled backward, putting hands behind her head, and gazed up at the fluffy clouds.

"You say you're not a wizard, but when it comes to magic, you seem to forget you're a bard. The fae are rightfully pretty skittish about bards because you can persuade us through your song and poetry, just as effectively as a Beguiler can reel in a human. Probably besting your bard skills was one of the reasons Sibyl came after you. She enjoyed the Challenge of conquering one thought immune to her charms."

"I don't think I was much of a challenge," said Logan, truthfully. He had been an easy conquest last fall.

Looking at a cloud in the shape of a rabbit, Brigit continued thinking out loud.

"Fae get bored easily. It's pretty common for us to do contests and wagers for the excitement alone. We need to give Sibyl a new Challenge, let's make her work for it."

"Are you sure you aren't a fae psychologist?"

Brigit took Logan's sarcasm at face value.

"No, I'm going to be a botanist. There's a disease in the trees back home that our fae talent can't cure. I'm hoping human science has the answer."

Faced with her truth, Logan took his time examining the dryad. However, she remained just as strange and mysterious as ever, especially when trying to explain her world to him.

Returning to her subject of the siren, Brigit said,

"We need something that would feed Sibyl's ego. That shouldn't be too hard. The more public, the better. She'll love losing if there's an audience."

"That makes no sense," said Logan, thoroughly confused. "Why would Sibyl love being publicly humiliated?"

"Because it increases her status. Unlike humans, winning isn't always the end goal. What we crave is the thrill. It's the process that toots our horn. It's one reason we seek so much human company. You're delightfully unpredictable."

"So from what you're describing that would mean the leaf mite at the Weberhaus enjoyed the beat-down you gave him?"

Brigit gave an exasperated sigh and climbed to her feet, dusting bits of grass off her jeans.

"In an odd way, it probably did. It was probably the most exciting thing that has happened to it in a decade. But overall, no, that was just a fight. If you're ever put into physical peril by the fae, respond quickly. You must meet them with just as much, if not more aggression. They'd kill you out of contempt if they thought you were weak."

Logan sat up, but he wasn't going to move more until he got some answers.

"Why did Sibyl try to poison you in the first place? Isn't that a Challenge? Why aren't you the one calling her out in a duel?"

Brigit didn't want to explain that Sibyl's attempt on her life was because the dryad was living in Logan's extra bedroom. She'd tell him the details some other time, just not today.

"I could Challenge Sibyl. Not to brag, but most likely I would win because I'm pretty cool like that. But I think you have the prior claim. If I got my Balance, would that free your heart?"

"Point taken."

"Don't look so serious. You'll win against Sibyl because I'm your bondmate. Remember, our bond is a pledge of assistance. An insult to you, is an insult to me."

Logan rose to his feet while Brigit continued talking.

"That's why Sibyl's prank was incredibly stupid. I've spent the last six months building a network of bond partners. I could ask all of those beings to assist us in our Challenge, which is also part of our problem. Because once Sibyl figures that out, we lose our advantage. By the way, I don't see any iron on your hands? What happened?"

"I had to get the rings I liked re-sized for my fingers. They should have them ready for me in about a week."

"Hm, all the more reason we should go visit the polo ponies."

"What?" asked Logan, confused.

"I talked with your welcome mat, but that silly being has a consciousness like a sieve. It's probably already forgotten all of my warnings."

"You talked to my welcome mat?" Logan's expression was incredulous.

"Sure. I talk to a lot of beings. Anyway, as I was saying, horses wear horseshoes, which are a great source of cheap iron. Horseshoes also hold a symbolic power too since they are an ancient form of protection. They would be a great item to place around your doors and windows."

"But that would stop you and the brownie also, wouldn't it?"

"The brùnaidh can cross as they have a resistance to iron due to their long association with humans. If you invite me, I can cross under iron, though it feels unpleasant. It's why you need to be very careful who you welcome through the door. Once they gain access, it's hard to evict them."

Chapter Nine
Sudden Death Chukker

Since neither Logan or Brigit knew where to find the stables, they went to the library for assistance. After getting directions, they found the bus that took an outside loop.

Scenery change from city buildings to green fields scattered with grazing farm animals. It felt like they were playing hooky from school and both, by wordless consent, talked about subjects other than the siren: teachers they liked and didn't, schedules that put you on opposite sides of the campus at nearly the same time, and the crazy long lines in administration.

The bus stop for the stables was at the base of a wide gravel drive. From the bottom of the hill, they could see three long green barns, decorated with white trim, at the top.

Walking up the drive, as they neared the barn, the heads of horses inside popped out the stall windows. As one, the animals turned to watch the two approach. Logan found the horse's silent stares unnerving.

"They aren't fae, are they?" he whispered to Brigit as if the animals could hear them.

"Of course not!" But even as she denied it, Brigit squinted her eyes, deciding to be on the lookout for any púca, such as the horse-shifting kelpies that enticed humans to ride on their backs.

As they came closer to the barn, Logan hesitated, wondering who they should ask for help. Meanwhile, Brigit sauntered confidently into one of the barns as if she owned the place.

The center aisle was paved in concrete and on each side was a row of stalls. Upon their entrance, the horses changed position so they could watch Brigit and Logan from behind the bars of their stall partitions.

Logan had no experience with horses but still found their silent observation disturbing although Brigit didn't seem to notice it. Instead, she stopped in front of each horse, silently observing the stall's occupant for several minutes before moving on to the next.

Eventually, she turned to Logan and told him, "We're in luck. It seems one of their herd mates threw a horseshoe at practice today, so the blacksmith is here. He's bound to have gobs of shoes."

Before they could seek the farrier, they were interrupted by a dramatic scene. Down the corridor, a large chestnut horse was rearing and letting out a piercing scream. The only person preventing the animal from bolting was a short woman holding onto a cotton lead rope attached to the horse's halter. While she was trying to calm the frightened animal, an older man, standing off to the side, was shouting and cursing at them both.

Logan turned to leave, not wanting to get involved, but Brigit muttered, "idiots" and trotted towards the disturbance. Changing direction, Logan followed, wondering what she planned on doing.

When she was within a few yards, Brigit dramatically raised her hand above her head as if calling for attention. Like a conjuring act, the cotton rope wriggled out of the sweaty hands of the groom and sailed through the air to land in Brigit's.

The dryad held the rope loosely, almost as if it didn't matter. Instead, all of Brigit's attention was for the panicked horse. The animal's pinned ears and rolling eyes showed a great deal of white. Even to Logan's uneducated eye, the horse seemed frightened out of its wits.

"Yes, I'll tell them," Brigit said out loud. "No one will hurt you again."

Brigit's calm, forthright manner seemed to convince the horse. He returned all four feet to the ground, his coat sweaty, and his body still shivering.

"Who are you, young lady?" demanded the man who had previously been shouting. "Who permitted you to be here? This is private property."

The man's attitude was so threatening and belligerent that Logan stepped between him and Brigit. While he didn't know how it happened, it was evident to Logan that Brigit had calmed the horse. Logan was just about to tell the man he should be grateful when they were interrupted.

During the excitement, a newcomer had arrived at the barn. He had run down the aisle from the opposite direction. He was an older man, with short salt-and-pepper hair and an athletic physique garbed in tan riding breeches, tall black boots, and a crisp white shirt.

Upon his arrival, the horse's handler stepped away as if she didn't want to be involved in what was about to happen.

"What do you think you are doing, Foster?" the older man barked. "I told you to leave this horse alone today."

It seemed the belligerent man who had been shouting was Foster. He shoved his jaw forward, his face becoming redder under his poorly cut, shaggy brown hair.

"The farrier is here, and Scalawag needs that shoe back. As the barn manager, it's my job to get these horses looked after."

"And as their trainer, ultimately, the care of these horses is up to me," countered the other in a stern, cold tone.

Like many of the teachers and coaches at the university, the trainer's words were flavored underneath with German.

Brigit intervened again.

"His shoe was loose because he hooked it on the fence the night before. The struggle to get it free hurt his hind leg."

She pointed at the left rear leg, adding, "I don't know much about horses, but it's this area. Scalawag says it hurts especially when this man," Brigit pointed now at Foster, "kept trying to lift it too high."

The trainer gave a measuring glance up and down at Brigit, taking in her pointed ears. He grunted, "Fae, huh?" before taking the lead rope from Brigit's hand. Holding the horse, he started running his hand over the area where the woman had indicated. His hand stayed there for a moment, and finally said, "Some heat and swelling here."

He told the groom to call the vet for an appointment.

"Make sure she brings her portable x-ray and ultrasound equipment with her."

During all this, the barn manager had continued to fume but could say nothing against the senior authority of the horse trainer. Foster loudly stated that he had work to do even if others had time to play with the fairies.

He stomped away, while the female groom left to call the vet. Only Logan, Brigit, and the trainer remained behind with the horse.

The trainer ran a calloused hand down the neck of Scalawag. While he murmured soothing noises to him, the horse pushed his forehead into the man's chest, leaning into the trainer's protective arms like a child seeking comfort.

"How did you know?" Logan whispered to Brigit, but before the fae could explain, the trainer did.

"She talked to it, of course. It's why I knew she was telling the truth. The fae do not torment animals with lies. It's only the captain of my polo team that they choose to tease to distraction."

Brigit was quick to disavow any connection with the siren.

"I'm not here for humans. We just wanted some horseshoes."

The trainer nodded, understanding, for he knew of the old folkways.

"Victor is our farrier, and he's out behind barn two.

You can take whatever he is willing to give. Let him know that Herr Schubert stands good for you."

With the horse trainer's goodwill and directions, they found the farrier in his leather apron under a Linden tree. He was in the middle of shoeing a bay mare, so they politely waited until he finished. The use of Herr Schubert's name softened the man's hard countenance.

"Usually I just recycle the horseshoes by heating and pounding them back into shape," he said, pointing to the anvil on the back of his truck's tailgate. "However, just take what you want from my discard pile, and I'll charge it back to Herr Schubert."

He gave them a wink and left them to sort through the pile of iron on the ground. Brigit walked away from him and put her back against the big tree. The fae took a deep breath as she closed her eyes.

"Dive in, human. I'll chat with the Holy Lime tree, here."

The gigantic tree didn't look like the lime trees back home as it had no green fruit. Logan squatted and started to sort through the pile of horseshoes.

"What if they have nails?" he called over his shoulder to her.

"Nails are good. The older and more beat up they are, the better."

"Better for tetanus," muttered Logan.

Eventually, he sorted out six, brushing them somewhat clean so they wouldn't dirty up his backpack. He slid them into the large pocket, next to his textbooks.

The seventh horseshoe he found was more twisted and bent than the others. It also had a bar that ran across both points of the horseshoe. He was about to show it to Brigit when a voice made him stand up quickly, forgetting what he held.

"You just can't stay away from me, can you?"

The siren greeted Logan as she approached, her left arm entwined with that of her new cavalier. The polo team captain, Franco Sabbatini, had a moonstruck expression on his face, causing Logan to feel a wave of pity for the man. Franco was riding to a dismal end that he was still unaware of.

The closer Sibyl came to him, the more pressure Logan felt around his chest until he found could hardly breathe. Sweat beaded his forehead, and his heart was frantically jumping as much as that chestnut horse had earlier. His vision tilted and the dullness of his senses return. His mind struggled, panicked with fear, loathing, and desire all at once.

The siren's spell over him was as strong as ever. A good night's sleep had fooled him into thinking he was almost back to normal; Sibyl's appearance returned him to reality.

"Sure Sibyl," Brigit called back, "we came all this

way to see you and your new beau be all grabby in the hay."

Brigit hadn't moved from her tree. If anything she leaned further back, and her relaxed attitude displayed open contempt of the other fae.

"The birds tell me you have a bond debt to this human, wood sprite."

"No thanks to you, chickenpox." While Brigit's tone was that of one mildly exasperated, seeing Logan's pale countenance, she decided to act. "Because of your little stunt with the bog sprites, I pronounce Fiat, a Mark of Injury between the three of us."

"Three?" The siren stroked her long blond hair, flashing her eyelashes at Logan in an obvious Beguiling.

"Yes. Logan's my bondmate and whatever injures him, hurts me. Whatever hurts me, hurts my fellow bondmates."

"A bondmate with a human. Oh, I'm so scared!" Sibyl's light, fraudulent laugh rang through the yard.

"And all of the fae with bonds to me. You didn't think about that, you bird-brain twit, did you?"

Brigit's words made the siren pause. For the first time, Sibyl appeared nervous, but she continued with an air of defiance, "Nothing you or your bond partners will do can save him, dryad. He will always be mine."

As if to prove her point, she dropped Franco's arm

and came closer to where Logan stood. She beckoned the human with one long finger. Against his will, Logan felt his feet shuffle over to her while his brain screamed for him to run away.

"Maybe he'll save himself?" said Brigit acidly. "Have you ever thought of that, my fowl-feathered lack-wit?"

"Never crossed my mind," the siren purred.

Logan was now close enough that Sibyl brought her hand up to caress his cheek. The American struggled against her pull, his mind screaming to free itself. Some primal power for survival came howling to the fore. Feeling the weight in his hand, he brought his own to counter the fae's touch.

As their fingers made contact, Sibyl gave a piercing scream.

The farrier straightened up from his work to gape in astonishment, and all the polo ponies turned their heads to watch as the siren bolted. Sibyl ran down the hill giving shrill horse whinnies. Lost without her, Franco ran after her, calling Sibyl's name.

When the siren came to the polo field, she flew through the gate. Prancing about the grounds, she did odd hop-skipping gait in a random zig-zag pattern across the green.

The farrier was puzzled, and Logan bewildered. Meanwhile, Brigit was doubled over, howling so hard with laughter that she was causing herself to hiccup.

Only when the dryad got herself under control did the two men get an explanation.

"Sibyl touched iron which was bad enough, but it's a used horseshoe. She now has to travel the path the iron took when the horse had it."

The farrier looked down at the horseshoe Logan was holding. The unique bar across the diameter identified it to him.

"That's going to take a long time. The horse that wore that played the number two position just last week."

Brigit was gasping and hiccuping laughter while Logan cracked a smile, the first since the beginning of the spring semester.

Chapter Ten
Freefall

After the confrontation with Sibyl, Logan's life became very quiet over the next few weeks. He fell into a routine of taking a delicious breakfast fixed by the brownie. Brigit took the time for a morning conference and imparted words of wisdom on how to handle the fae before they went their separate ways.

Because of what happened at the polo barn he knew this was a false peace. However, Logan decided to enjoy what he had at the moment. The cloud over his emotions and mind was still there, but he was better able to function. Whenever he asked Brigit about the Sibyl problem (as she called it), the dryad assured him she was working on it.

Meanwhile, she introduced him to dozens of different fae students. These were beings of all types, some with little human resemblance, but all were fascinating to Logan. The fae students were all associated with her through what she called the Laws of Civility. The favors and exchanges were almost too numerous for him to understand.

Logan learned a delicate diplomacy that committed him to nothing.

He was expecting Brigit one afternoon when Logan heard a knock on the door. While touching the iron horseshoe hanging over the door, he peered through the peephole. A delivery man, garbed in a short-sleeved pullover in trademark colors of black and red, with a baseball cap pulled over his eyes, was standing outside.

"Dinnae open it," came a warning whisper from the kitchen, but Logan thought he knew what to do - stay behind the threshold. Even Brigit was only able to cross under the iron horseshoes hanging over the door because he had given permission.

"Only someone living here can sign for the package," instructed the delivery driver, holding the electronic pad and stylus away from Logan's reaching hands. He was tall, with broad shoulders and a trim build as if he worked out a lot at the gym.

"I live here," Logan confirmed.

"Okay, if ye're sure but don't say I dinnae ask ye," said the courier, as he flipped a long braid of black hair over his shoulder. When handing over the pad the deliveryman was scrupulous in his manner, and avoided touching Logan's fingers which bore two iron rings, one on each hand.

The student gave a scribble and returned the pad before reaching for the parcel. Logan wondered what care package his mom had sent this time.

When his fingers touched the box, the lights went out. The floor dropped out from underneath him. Like in dreams, Logan plunged downward into a dark void.

Logan was in free fall, cold air brushing his arms and face as he plummeted through a black tunnel. Falling seemed to last forever, yet it took just a moment before he hit butt first on a hard surface. Instinctively, he splayed out his hands to steady himself, feeling something cold and smooth under his palms.

He groaned, stumbling to his feet. Something fae had taken him. What an idiot he had been!

As Logan wondered where he was, the chamber brightened from dark to gray. The illumination was slow and gradual, like the sun rising on the horizon. The light revealed he was standing in someone's bedroom, most likely that of a girl, if the decor was stereotypically correct.

There was a wooden desk and chair, a bookshelf stuffed with books, and a large bed at the end of the chamber. Oddly enough, the room lacked any sign of color; everything was in shades of white, gray, black, or a dull brown.

His first step was tentative but discovering the ground under his feet didn't disappear, Logan explored. The light came from a sponge-like fungus clustered in metal cages mounted on the smooth stone walls. As he approached them, the light grew brighter, almost as if it sensed his presence. When he moved away, they became dimmer.

The walls were stone but had a rough natural texture, like the interior of a cave. A sort of soft plaster or paint in an off-white color coated the surface.

Next, Logan examined the desk and bookshelf. The furniture was beautiful and ornate, with a relief of leaves and acorns decorating the chair back and its legs. When he ran his hand across the surface of the wood, it was worn smooth from age. Oddly, it was slightly warm and gave off a feeling of comfort as he touched it.

Besides the furniture giving emotion, there was also something unusual about their construction. It took several minutes for Logan to figure what made them different: the furniture had not been cut, carved, and nailed together. Instead, their structure had been shaped, perhaps grown, into its end form.

On the desk, he found a few human books, mostly technical volumes about plant biology and chemistry. Opening up a book on tree and plant identification, Logan discovered highlighted pages with scribbled notes in the margin. However, it was in a script he didn't recognize. It proved he was away from the Bewachterberg translation magic because the images remained indecipherable.

The bookshelf contained so many volumes they were stacked in double rows. Logan randomly pulled one off the shelf, finding it different than the ones lying on the desk.

He ran his hand over the book's cover to feel a rough, bumpy, irregular material, like a handwoven fiber similar to linen or silk. The pages were thicker than regular paper, and the characters looked to have been inked by hand. It was more like a journal than a printed book, but since he couldn't read the scribbles, its subject remained a mystery.

The book in his hands started to become warmer. When it wriggled, he hastily put it back on the shelf.

"We're not in Kansas anymore."

As far as he knew, Logan had never visited the Perilous Realm before. He believed he could no longer claim that distinction.

He turned, looking around the room again, trying

to decide what to do next. The only other pieces of furniture left to investigate was a bed and a tall wardrobe cabinet.

He examined the armoire and discovered it was another piece of grown furniture, as the doors were not straight but flowed with the grain of the wood. The silver cabinet pulls were in the form of hands.

Recalling a childhood story, Logan opened the wardrobe and reaching between the hanging garments touched the back of it. Disappointingly, it was solid and did not lead to another world, preferably his own.

Pulling his hand out, Logan examined the clothes. They were hanging on thick twisted vines serving as hangers and were just as strange as everything else.

All of them were in neutral colors such as white, silver-gray, or black. They had no seams or zippers, though a few had laces or buttons. The material itself was the strangest of all: it appeared to be nothing but spiderwebs, moss, or leaves.

One dress started whispering, and when a sleeve came up to caress his face, Logan quickly stepped back and shut the wardrobe doors.

The bed was the last thing he investigated. It was a thick bulky mattress, more like a stuffed bag as there were no springs inside.

Hanging from hooks in the ceiling was an opaque veil. It surrounded the bed as a decorative curtain, and the fabric was rough, raw silk. Pulling back one of the drapes, it revealed a quilted bedspread, composed of a pattern of black and white diamond shapes.

The coverlet and pillows were neatly in order, and at the head of the bed was propped up a doll about the length of Logan's forearm. It was a plump figure of a tree with leaves on its head, branches for arms, and roots for legs. The stuffed toy appeared shabby and well-worn.

Logan yawned, suddenly feeling tired. He didn't know how much time had passed, but everyone knew the Perilous distorted it. Thinking of the Goldilocks story, he kicked off his shoes and climbed onto the bed. Under his weight, the mattress crackled and squished, but it was not unpleasant.

"Sorry, buddy," he told the teddy-tree as he moved it to the other side and laid down.

He yawned again, closing his eyes.

Whoever brought him here would appear sooner or later.

Logan woke up to weight on his chest.

The anvil was a black cat with eyes like candle flames. They were bright yellow with dark red pupils which Logan found hypnotic.

"Where is Brigit?" The being's voice was raspy.

Logan's hand, lifting to pet the creature, stopped in mid-air. For a moment, he had forgotten he was in the

Perilous. Realizing he had broken one of Brigit's cardinal rules and let a fae get within reach, he tried to play it cool.

"I don't know a Brigit."

The cat narrowed its eyes. Its body was an unmoving stone except for its long black tail whipping angrily back and forth over Logan's hips.

"Don't play games with me, human. Her father is going to be here at any moment. It would be to your advantage if you coughed up the truth. Start first with why you are in her bedroom."

That didn't sound good on several counts, but Logan was stubbornly loyal, sometimes to the point of foolishness.

"I'm not going to tell you where she is or how to find her."

The fae beast started taking a bath. Logan, who had grown up with cats, recognized the tactic. It was a self-soothing procedure, giving cats time to consider things.

"She's truly okay," Logan sat up as he reassured the being. "But I don't think I can tell you any more than that. Sorry."

The cat paused in its licking to give him an assessing stare. Before Logan could say anything further, an opening formed on the wall at the other end of the room. The aperture of swirling shadows swelled until it settled into the form of a gaping hole.

Stepping through the doorway was a powerfully built dark-skinned man. The newcomer was broad as a linebacker in his shoulders and chest. His baldness lent severeness to the angles of his face, enhancing his fierce scowl.

He wore an outfit vaguely reminiscent of the Elizabethan Renaissance. The loose, cotton shirt was under an embroidered wool and leather doublet with intricately slashed sleeves. His hose showed off muscular legs and a leather belt, wrapped twice around his waist, held a scabbard and sword.

His imposing style was assisted by four fae, two women and two men, who stood behind him. They also wore swords.

Chapter Eleven
Meet the Parents

Where is my daughter Brigit?" the newcomer demanded in a powerful baritone. The books on the shelves fluttered in agitation.

Logan stood up slowly, trying to buy time. While he wondered how much trouble he was in, the cat snickered behind the paw it was using to clean its whiskers.

"She's well, sir," said Logan, hastily putting his sneakers back on. "Would you like me to take a message to her?"

The dark eyes, so like his daughter's, did not seem to take Logan's attempt at appeasing his temper well. Instead, he barked, "Come here!" gesturing for the young man to come closer.

Logan approached but was careful to stay at least an arm's length away from the fae he faced. The being looked him up and down in a dismissive manner while sniffing the air as if he just discovered a displeasing odor. While his massive size was unlike the short, wiry build of his daughter's, his dismissing manner reminded Logan strongly of Brigit.

"Did you seduce my daughter with your silver tongue, bard? Like your kind always do?"

"Ur. Hm. We're just friends."

"Worse and worse."

Brigit's father put his hands on his hips, surveying him. While they were standing face to face, the sword in its scabbard rattled, trying to leap out into the grip of its master. As if it was a guard dog, the fae patted it and told the weapon to settle down.

He looked over his shoulder at those who accompanied him and told them, "This is why I told her to ignore the human lands. Visiting there always brings trouble. Now we have this human beguiler to deal with."

Remembering Brigit's warnings about meeting fae, Logan said, "Being a bard, you know I can discern the truth. Fae Glamour has no hold over me."

"What do you take me for? A seedling?" the fae snorted in exasperation. "Of course, I know that. It makes you being here, instead of my daughter, doubly unsettling. She's an impulsive, friendly child. If you've taken advantage of her, I'll make sure you regret it."

Logan couldn't imagine Brigit allowing anyone to take advantage of her and was about to say so when they were interrupted. Someone was shoving past the four guards, crying out in a high feminine voice, "Is she here!? Is she home!?"

"No, dear," said Brigit's father, grimacing. "That stupid siren got it all wrong. Our Summoning magic caught only this worthless human. However, it does seem to know our daughter."

The fae woman coming to stand beside Brigit's father was clearly her mother. She had the same nose, forehead, and jawline with the generous, smiling mouth of her offspring. However, her skin wasn't that toffee brown of Brigit's but was a gray-olive color. Her dark thick hair was smooth, showing only a hint of a wave.

Her dress was also Elizabethan in style. The shiny gown embroidered with silver wire had accents of pearls the size of robin eggs. Spun spiderweb made the ruff around her neck, complete with a working spider about the size of Logan's palm.

Spoiling the historical effect of the outfit was a diadem sitting on top of her head made of modern Christmas tinsel.

Upon seeing Logan, her smile died away. After an open-mouthed gasp of "Not a bard!" she buried her face in her husband's bicep and started to weep loudly.

The spider scrambled to find a spot without losing its place when Brigit's father placed an arm around her shaking shoulders to comfort her. He glared over the top of the tinsel at Logan.

"Now, look at what you've done."

Logan felt horrible.

The cat jumped off the bed and took a spot beside Logan's foot. The creature said in a rasping, mocking tone, "Look at what you did now, human. You made the queen cry. Boohoo."

"I didn't think the fae could cry," Logan whispered back, under his breath.

Brigit's father explained to her mother, "Remember, dear, bards are always looking for a free meal or some enchanted gift from the Perilous. Our daughter is too smart to lose her heart to one."

If his words were an attempt to calm her they failed, for the fae woman's wailing increased in volume. The four attendants shuffled nervously, looking away. The cat directed its next words of sarcasm to the king.

"Smart move, my liege, in reminding Queen Elixia her harp was stolen by a bard the last time a human beguiler visited our kingdom."

As she cried harder little snowflakes, bits of spitting snow, emerged from her eyes to drift into the air.

"I don't want another poet cluttering up the realm! I want our daughter back!"

It took some effort on the part of the king, but after wiping away more icy snowflakes, Queen Elixia was able to compose herself.

"Throw him back," she told her bondmate. "I have enough on my hands hosting that arrogant wraith of your sister."

The king sighed and reminded her, "The wraith is acting as a diplomat from Queen Titania, sweetheart. Let's keep the family peace and not insult it."

"It's always judging me, reporting every slight and cobweb back to your dear cousin."

The snowflakes returned. The king nodded towards Logan, trying to change the subject.

"Perhaps this bard's silver-tongue can amuse the wraith. After all, the diplomat was once human, so perhaps they'll find something in common to discuss tonight at your evening party. Humans can be entertaining. Especially bards."

Queen Elixia frowned, seemingly not impressed by what she saw when looking at Logan. She leaned closer to her bondmate and said in a stage whisper, "If he isn't amusing, can I lock him in a cloven tree and let his screams entertain us?"

"See, my dear. There are always options," the king replied.

The four tall, handsome beings with very pointy swords forced Logan to follow behind Brigit's parents. The black cat trotted alongside, keeping pace.

After exiting Brigit's bedroom, they entered a tunnel carved out of the rock. Sconces mounted on the wall, holding more of the sponge lights, illuminated their way.

At a branch off, they turned left, coming through an area of the cave where the ceiling was as tall as a cathedral's. Hanging stalactites, taller than Logan, glittered and winked like white diamonds in the dim light. The young man slowed to admire them only to receive a jostle by one of his escorts to hurry. By pausing, they had increased the distance between them and the king and queen.

The couple's voices floated back to him, echoing in the cavern. They were discussing the merits of changing the dinner party from an Elizabethan theme to some other human era. Perhaps the Greeks? Togas were so much more comfortable than farthingales and perhaps the sheet-like draping might flatter the wraith?

Being jogged along, no one ever touching his hands and their iron, Logan was close enough to hear more about the wraith. How to entertain Titania's diplomat was more of a problem as neither of their majesties could think of something that might appeal to it. It seemed Queen Titania's ambassador was a stick-in-the-mud. It didn't like party games and answered all attempts at conversation with depressing monosyllables. Elaborate entertainments designed to please it fell flat.

"Is a wraith like a ghost?" Logan asked the cat.

"Pretty much. Like all wraiths, it results from a human's death. It must have died in the Perilous Realm and become trapped here. Queen Titania probably sent it as her ambassador to avoid playing favorites amongst her fae nobles. Regardless, it was a poor choice as it's a wet blanket."

A cooling draft became stronger as they started on an upward slope. Suddenly, the group emerged into an outdoor landscape, and Logan looked behind him to see where they had exited.

At first glance, it appeared to be the base of a mountain. But the boulders, waterfalls, and vegetation were all too perfect, too artistically arranged to be natural, even though the color palette was still dreary. The presence of flapping banners and crystal glass windows was further evidence that the mound was not of an organic origin.

Once again, his companions nudged Logan. They broke into a jog to catch up to the royal couple.

It looked like the dinner party would be an outdoor event. They continued down a well-defined path through a grove of trees.

The forest was awe-inspiring and majestic in size,

rivaling the giants of the Sequoia forest back home. However, instead of those familiar red trunks, these trees gave off a phosphorus white-silver glow that had a faint gray mottling underneath the glitter. The trunks were fluted and ridged columns with a surface that appeared as smooth as glass though Logan didn't dare touch them. The branches were high over their heads, and they must have been brittle; when they moved the leaves made a tinkling sound like jingle bells.

Suddenly, the forest opened to a small meadow where the queen's evening party was already in progress. Word must have gotten out about the Queen's change of plans as half the group was attired in togas, while some still in doublets and hose.

For the royal couple, their attire had changed: they now wore flowing white robes, with snakes serving as belts, and laced sandals. Surprised, Logan looked down to find he wore the same. A garland of bay leaves was around his head.

At their arrival, everyone stood, giving bows, curtsies, or salutes as their majesties passed them. Logan was brought out of the procession by one of the guards who pushed him down into a seat. The chair seemed similar to what Logan had seen in Brigit's room but was more ornate.

His seat put him opposite, but far away, from the royals.

The cat jumped on the table beside Logan. Its head swiveled to watch as the king and queen took their seats.

"I wonder if you will enjoy being tonight's entertainment?"

Despite the fae being's comments, Logan was glad to have someone that spoke to him for the silence of the guards had been unnerving.

It seemed no one but the cat was interested in his presence so Logan felt free to look about with open curiosity.

While some had changed the style of their dress, the decor of the banquet remained medieval. The serving tables were set up in a square and decorated with silver candlesticks, candles, and topiaries of mythical beasts.

A servant approached and placed a silver plate and a diamond-encrusted goblet in front of the college student. A bounty of silverware, with knives, forks, and spoons was laid out in front of him, until there was no clear space on the white tablecloth.

"The queen likes a lot of shiny things. Usually it's expensive stuff. Except for that shiny plastic headpiece thing she is wearing. That is utter trash. Who is dressing her these days I cannot imagine."

Contemplating the three goblets set in front of it for its amusement, the cat took its time to make a decision. Savoring the pleasure, it knocked one of them off the table onto the grass.

Logan's stomach growled as the food started to arrive. However, as the server placed it before him, he looked down with disappointment.

It was just a gray lump.

The young man mashed it around with his fork to make it appear like he had eaten some of it. Besides, he knew he shouldn't eat it. Everyone knew the stories.

"With all the fables of the fae hospitality, I expected the food to be a bit grander," confided Logan to his companion.

"Don't blame your hostess," hissed the cat, displeased. "Being a bard, our Glamour holds no sway over your vision. You're stuck seeing the truth of it all so blame your talent, not our hospitality."

The truth was the real fairy world held a lot of blandness.

It was like seeing a world through a black and white TV with a lot of monochromatic grays. Everything was a blend of gray porridge.

The attendee's apparel (or in some cases lack of) was bizarre. However, it was the weirdness of their visages, some funnily strange and others terrifying, which captured most of Logan's attention.

But even these interesting beings started to pale in interest as the dinner dragged and Logan found himself growing tired.

"The true nature of the Perilous is that of a flat place, with little variation or color," the cat said, knocking over a second goblet.

"While you have wisely not tasted the food set before you, I will attest to its dullness. It holds no flavor, no spice. This is the nature of the Perilous."

"Brigit mentioned something about that," said Logan, trying to hide his yawn with the back of his hand. Why was he so tired? "She said the fae love Challenges and didn't mind losing. I didn't understand it at the time. I still don't."

"Oh, we mind losing if you do it badly. By badly, I mean, if is tedious and without showmanship. Bore us and you will find yourself chopped up into tiny little bits your mother wouldn't recognize, and cast to the four winds."

"Why not shop in the human lands for clothes, furniture, and stuff like that?"

"Unfortunately, anything brought from the human lands to the Perilous eventually absorbs the characteristics of our home. You'll become as flat as that wraith over there sitting next to their majesties."

The cat pointed its paw to a faceless ghost, somewhat translucent, sitting at the chair placed to the right of the king. Shocked at the cat's statement, Logan quickly looked at his own hands. He was relieved to find them warmly pink.

"Of course, its been here for a few thousand years,

so it might take a few months for you to see the change," mused the cat, knocking the third goblet off the table.

"In the long run, it's cheaper and easier to travel a portal to the human lands. Play with them a while until we tire of the game. When this dinner finishes, I plan to hunt mice in the human lands where things are colorful, unpredictable, and amusing."

"I don't think that is why Brigit —" Logan stopped himself before revealing Brigit's location or her purpose.

The cat was far too smart.

"It was assumed the princess fled to the human lands," the cat-being said smugly. "We all knew she longed to go, but her parents refused to hear of it. They believed she was too young to live among you weird, unpredictable creatures. Their concern sprang from love, though their arguments did not persuade their daughter to stay."

"Did she tell them why she wanted to go?"

"Certainly. To save our trees, she said. She's almost as dramatic as her mother. And her moods can be as variable as our queen."

The cat narrowed its eyes.

"You claim to know Brigit well, but I find that hard to believe."

"I've known her for a couple of months. Human time that is," explained Logan. "She has a lot of friends, so her parents needn't worry."

"Friends?" The cat hissed again, this time in surprise.

"I meant to say bondmates. People she hangs out with that are like her. Other fae."

"I know what friends are, you idiot." Offended, the cat looked off in the distance. It took a few moments for its outraged fur to settle before it continued the discussion. "My doubt that you know our princess increases."

"I do know her!" Being a bard who valued truth, Logan was incensed that anyone would doubt his word. "She introduced me to one of her bondmates who got rid of some monsters living in my apartment. Since then she's been helping me with a siren which Beguiled me."

The cat's eyes, which had been slit, now opened wide, better to reveal their dancing flames. Its whiskers seemed to have increased in length and were on high alert.

"There must be more to this story. I do not see why Brigit would help you, a human, out of such a mess."

"She owes me a Debt of Gratitude."

Cats do not like to be surprised, and it hissed.

"Don't tell that to her parents. Unless you want to live here forever and a day."

"They can't harm me. Brigit said that would be a cowardly act."

"For the one that holds the Bond, yes. Not for extended family. You will discover it's a flexible code."

The cat's eyes closed again. Its whiskers relaxed as it purred.

"I have to agree with the king. You do have the potential to entertain. And I'd recommend you be very entertaining. The more you please them with your silver-tongue, the more likely you will return to the human lands in one piece."

"Brigit said wagers, duels, love affairs, gossip, anything that alleviates the tedium of the Perilous Realm would interest the fae. Does that hold for their majesties?"

"Drama always appeals," reminded the cat.

Before they could speak again, the tree leaves above them gave a ringing cascade of chimes, signaling the end of the main meal and the arrival of dessert. Servants hustled about, delivering slices of cake on porcelain plates so thin that they were almost as transparent as glass.

Seeing the meal was coming to an end and fearing to lose his opportunity, Logan jumped to his feet and shouted, "I'd like to lay a wager with the king."

At his pronouncement, the audience became silent. All eyes and, for those without eyes, heads, swiveled to him.

"I wager that I know more about Brigit Cullen, than her father, the king."

Chapter Twelve
The Wager

The king summoned the bard to stand before his table.

"What wager do you propose?"

"Let the cat ask us three questions about Brigit, but only the Brigit of today, not her childhood or something I wouldn't know," said Logan, trying to eliminate loopholes where the fae could take advantage.

"If I give answers better than your majesty, I shall be returned to the human land, at the same time and place that I left. That me and mine cannot be harmed at any time during or after the bet is in play."

The king looked over to his wife, who was clapping

her hands in excitement.

"Amusing enough? Shall I accept?" At the nod of her head, the king turned to the assembly and announced, "I accept this human's wager. If I win, the human must take me immediately to my missing daughter. Do you agree?"

Logan nodded, his hands growing sweaty. He knew how horrible getting lectures from your parents could be and wanted to spare Brigit her father's unexpected arrival.

The king continued speaking to his court. "Jib, the cat púca, will act as an arbitrator. So there are no accusations of favoritism, Queen Titania's wraith will serve as the judge."

At the announcement, the black cat jumped down from the table. It swaggered past Logan, waving its tail. When it passed the man, it said, "I'm not going to go easy on you, kid. You'll have to win fairly."

With the wager in place, there was a rush to place bets. Jib yowled when it discovered that, as an arbitrator, it couldn't participate.

"I should be able to bet on the human. No one else is!" the cat cried at the perceived injustice. "I mean the odds are fantastic! I would make a killing if this boy won."

"Since you are asking the questions, it wouldn't be right. You could slant the outcome in your favor," explained the queen as she collected gold and silver coins, handfuls of acorns, and a few diamonds and pearls from her subjects.

"Stupid rules," hissed the púca, its hair standing up in displeasure.

"The wraith can't bet either," Queen Elixia pointed out.

The cat stared angrily at the floating ghost.

After the bets were placed, the king held up a hand. He requested silence so the competition could begin.

"My first question is," began Jib, who strolled casually back and forth across the queen's table, "where is our princess currently living?"

Before he could plan a strategy, Logan rushed to speak. "The human lands."

The king gave him a condescending look.

"Hochstrasse 2389, Geheimetür, Bewachterberg, in the human lands."

The leaves in the tree canopies above them chimed. One leaf floated down to land in front of the king's feet.

"The first round goes to the king," announced the wraith in a thready whisper, causing the audience to lean forward to hear. Once they realized who won, there was a round of applause.

"Better luck next time, human," the cat said to Logan.

The smugness of the king's expression irritated

Logan. He leaned forward, hands clasped hard behind him, to hear the next question.

"Second round. What is the favorite human food of our princess?"

Behind the king, the queen gestured wildly, silently mouthing a word. Jib hissed. "There will be no assistance from the audience."

The queen's attempt to aid her bondmate didn't matter because he hadn't understood what she had tried to tell him. However, like many parents, the king believed he knew his offspring.

He responded with a confident uttering of "Cake."

Logan knew he had jumped the last question. He needed to use his talent for recognizing the truth. Thinking over all the things he had seen Brigit eat, he tried different words on his tongue.

Only one word tasted right.

"Chocolate."

The trees rattled again, but this time one of their leaves fell to the ground next to Logan's sneakers. The wraith announced the human as the winner of the second round.

"How could you get that one wrong?" the queen wailed.

The púca did not like being upstaged. It started to hack as if coughing up a hairball. The royal court quieted in dreadful anticipation. When the True Beast stopped its retching, an audible sigh went around the court.

"My last question, which will decide the winner, is," the cat made a dramatic pause, wrapping a tail around its forepaws, "what was the real reason for Brigit left the Perilous realm?"

"Everyone knows why she left - it was the trees," called out someone from the court.

"She thought human science could help," said another.

However, the queen shouted to her husband, "Remember, love, the last question is always a trick!"

After the upset of the second question, she was not going to play strictly by the rules.

Nevertheless, the king could not think of an answer that wasn't the obvious one. His daughter made an irritating habit of telling anyone that would listen before she left what her goal was. She desired human advice on the disease destroying many of the groves.

It was never a secret.

Logan closed his eyes and steadied himself by breathing deeply through his nose. All he had to do was find the truth by tasting it on his tongue.

Yes, Brigit wanted help for saving her beloved trees. That tasted like truth, but it didn't feel like the full truth. It gave him a slight tang on his tongue, but the answer lacked the full richness that absolute truth gave Logan.

He thought of Brigit, her quick, bright nature, her

intelligence, but also her traits of needing Balance in all she did. He thought about what little he had observed of her parents, and he thought of his own parents. Their love, as well as their impatience with him, when he decided Bewachterberg was where he wanted to attend university.

"Being a cat, I have the patience to wait all day. However, perhaps the contestants could answer before the court expires from boredom?"

The king answered first.

"Our royal daughter wanted to discover a cure for the disease killing our trees."

While a murmur was heard in the branches, no leaf fell.

The lack of response caused an air of nervous tension amongst the audience, and even the queen held her breath. He was a human bard; what he said was bound to make the dinner memorable.

Logan felt the exciting and dangerous exhilaration of not knowing if he would win or lose. At this moment, he understood the fae; their obsession for passion and color in their lives.

"Brigit left because her parents refused to listen. She left because the queen and king had no faith in her. They refused to trust her judgment and integrity."

Vehemently whipping their branches in enthusiasm; the trees sounded as if a sudden windstorm had come upon them.

Two leaves fell - one at the king's feet and another by Logan's.

The young man bent to pick up the silver leaf, feeling a slight frost burn in his fingers as he touched it.

"It will be up to the wraith to decide this tie-breaker," decided Jib.

This time it was to the wraith that all eyes and heads turned. The wraith seemed to sense the interest from the crowd, for it twisted a bit as if turning. The column of the gray-white ghost floated up from its position behind the table. Its face had long been worn away and what remained of its features was thin, barely there, and mostly see-through.

Its thin, quivering whisper forced everyone to silence so they could hear what was about to be said.

"I can barely remember the sensation of being human. Of caring. Of the desire to fit in, and the desire to stand out." The wraith paused in its speech, the column of wisp wavering in the breeze.

"This is the first time since my arrival any have been interested in what I would say. Being here, I have felt the crushing feeling of not being listened to."

Logan could feel it. Could feel what was about to happen.

"The human has spoken the correct answer."

Logan smiled just as the world came crashing down on his head.

When Brigit came up the stairs, she immediately noticed the opened door. Laying across the threshold was an arm.

"Logan!"

Welcome, Brigit!

But the fae had no time for exchanging civilities with the coco mat. She put her fingers over Logan's neck, feeling for a pulse. His skin felt clammy and slightly damp. His long brown lashes lay starkly against skin that was paler than usual.

"So this is where you live now?"

Startled, Brigit looked up from Logan's limp form to see a familiar black cat staring at her with eyes of orange and red flame.

"Jib! Did you hurt Logan?" Brigit demanded. She looked down the hallway and seeing it vacant, stepped over the threshold. Grabbing Logan by the ankles, she dragged him into the safety of the apartment.

"Is that how you greet long lost friends?" asked the cat. The True Beast settled down on the welcoming coco mat, tucking its front paws under its body.

Welcome! I cannot tell you if they are home today. But you may wait.

Brigit ignored the cat and the mat while she lifted the unconscious Logan to a sitting position on the floor. The woman put his arm around her shoulders and brought him to standing but even with her fae strength, lifting his limp form was difficult.

She half-carried, half-dragged him to the living room couch. Laying him down, she brought his feet up onto the cushions before rushing off to get him a wet washcloth from the bathroom.

"Hallo? Remember me?" Jib called after her. "Why don't you invite me in so we can chat more easily? The iron over the door is preventing me from being your guest."

Not until Brigit was satisfied that Logan was resting as comfortably as she could make him, did she address the cat.

"Did you have anything to do with this?" At her tone, Jib rolled onto its side, showing a furry stomach, while it nonchalantly licked a paw with extended claws.

"Don't get so worked up, princess."

"Don't call me that. Especially around here." She put her hands on hips, asking again, "Did you have something to do with this?"

"A siren sent message birds to several kingdoms asking if anyone had misplaced a wood sprite. With an address, your parents sent a Summons to bring you home, but bagged a human instead."

During the cat's recitation, Brigit thumped a fist against the threshold to accent the word that exploded from her lips, "Idiots!"

"The Summons was addressed to Occupant. Does he live here with you? How unusual."

The cat's red irises flickered wildly with curiosity.

"I know you'll never shut up unless we talk, but can we have this discussion inside."

As she walked to the doorway she automatically picked up the bay laurel wreath that had fallen off of Logan's head. Underneath it she discovered a silver leaf. Brigit gave a quick exhalation as she picked it up. Touching it made a wave of homesickness wash over her. She tucked it in her pocket and turned back to Jib who was watching her with avid interest.

The dryad gave the True Beast a formal invitation, outlining the boundaries and rules. While she talked, the cat gave a long stretch to its back before casually sauntering inside, flicking the very top tip of its tail. Brigit closed the door behind it and returned to the living room to check on Logan.

"He's got a touch of Fae Fever from being in the Perilous Realm," said the púca. "He'll shake it off in a day or so. A bit of bone broth would do him good."

"Haud yer wheesht! He needs only what I be making him, Mr. Nosy," said a female voice from the kitchen.

"A brùnaidh? Brigit, you are living better than a queen. Even your mother can't get a brownie."

"Hush, Jib, have some respect."

"Ah, a moggy has no' respect, so dinnae try to

150

make a hat from a bundle of straw."

"Whatever is she talking about, Brigit? Can she not speak the Queen's Fae?"

Brigit hissed at the cat again to shut up, but as Logan's eyelids had started to flicker, she was distracted from more reproaches.

"Am I back in Kansas now?" the young man asked.

"What? Kansas, where's that?" asked Brigit, but she received no reply. Logan was still too disoriented; Jib had wandered off to inspect the bedrooms; and the brownie had disappeared.

Logan was struggling to sit up, so Brigit pulled him sideways with a hand under his elbow, stuffing pillows behind his back. From clammy, his skin had grown very hot.

Fae Fever made a healthy human feel like they had altitude sickness. But Brigit worried Logan could suffer severe repercussions. Being Beguiled by the siren had weakened his immune system, leaving him too vulnerable.

Brigit didn't have enough experience to know what she should do. She'd need expert help.

"Do you think you can walk to your bedroom?"

Logan nodded his head, but it flopped a bit drunkenly making the fae woman skeptical. But between his weak assistance and Brigit's fae strength, she got him to his bed. They almost tripped over Jib. The cat flopped in the middle of the floor right in their path.

"Cold," Logan muttered, fretfully pulling at the comforter.

Jib jumped up on the bed and gave Logan a critical eye.

"Dehydrated."

"Thanks, Dr. Jib," replied Brigit sarcastically. She didn't know why Logan was wearing a toga. The white draping looked thin, so she collected an extra blanket she had seen in the closet to drape over him. After reassuring Logan she'd be right back, she went to the kitchen. The brownie handed her a sports water bottle.

"The laddie is looking pretty peely wally. Here's a wee bit of melted sugar and a hauf of whiskey. Dinnae tell the moggy but, aye, a bit of soup would do him good too."

"Thanks," said Brigit gratefully, feeling overwhelmed. "I need to get word to my friend Celia. She's a naiad, training to be a nurse. I can't use a phone, so I'll have to go to her apartment. But I don't feel I can leave him alone."

"Aff with ye. I'll look after the wee laddie till ye return."

"I'll take Jib with me. I don't know why it's here or what it's up to."

"That be best, methinks. I'll look after the laddie while ye be gone."

The brownie's unusual suggestion startled Brigit. Brownies did not involve themselves with the personal care of the householder. However, she was too grateful to question the gesture. Collecting her wallet, she grabbed a protesting Jib by its neck and left for help.

Chapter Thirteen
As the Crow Flies

rs. Tiggy, is that you?"

"Tis is, laddie. Tis is. No' drink it all up, like a good lad."

Logan's hand shook as the sun-browned hairy hand steadied the cup at his lips.

"I had the strangest dream," he said, sinking back onto the pillows under his head.

"I'm sure ye did," muttered the brownie. She awkwardly patted the top of his hand and set the empty soup bowl on the side table.

"There was a king and a queen. And a talking cat. Do you think I'll meet him again? I like cats."

"Most likely, barra, but tis time to sleep."

"Okay, Mrs. Tiggy."

Logan snuggled down under the covers while the brownie sang him a Scottish lullaby.

In a golden cradle on a quiet floor
Under the branches of trees, and the wind rocking it
Sleep child, and sleep safe

The brownie had agreed to Brigit's scheme since she recognized Logan's last name. Well, if she was asked by the Great Queen how the lad got to such a pass, she could at least honestly tell Badb Catha she had done her best.

The dryad was tempted to travel by jumping from tree to tree, as it would make a fast trip to Celia's apartment complex. But Jib could only travel through trees with portals and there were none near where she wanted to go.

Not for the first time, Brigit wished she could use cell phones. If she could handle the tech, she wouldn't be sitting on a public bus, looking like a crazy person as she talked to an invisible púca.

"Now I know why my six older siblings left home ages ago," she said sideways out of her mouth to Jib. When a human sitting in front of her turned to give a sad pitying look, Brigit stopped herself from rudely displaying her middle finger.

"The human was adequate to the task and saved

himself," said Jib. "Why are you upset?"

The cat was standing on its hind legs, front paws on the window glass, taking in the town scenery. Jib was a púca and being a True Beast, could only remain in a feline form, unlike the kelpie.

"I already owe a Debt of Gratitude to him. What my parents did just made the responsibility greater."

It had been only a matter of time before her parents caught up with her. However, Brigit had been optimistic, thinking she would be in her senior year by the time they found her. She never thought others might be dragged into the dispute, especially not someone she already owed a Debt of Gratitude.

Jib left the window and sat down next to Brigit, purring.

"You can't blame your parents for wanting to know where you are. You did take off rather abruptly. We were all worried."

"I left a note," snapped Brigit, "I'm not heartless."

"Have you ever thought that leaving the Perilous without permission from their majesties flaunted the Law of Civility? Other fae have been exiled for less."

"Exile me then. Big loss." Brigit crossed her arms and looked away, her eyes misty. At her show of distress, Jib put a paw on her hand and Brigit reflexively stroked its fur.

"That's why you need a diplomatic, smooth talker like me. I can help soften them to your way of thinking. Besides, Bewachterberg looks interesting. I could stay awhile. Keep an eye on you while you remain in the human lands."

"Not likely, Jib. They're stubborn. It's why I stopped trying to get them to listen."

Brigit stood up, picking the cat up to cradle it in her arms against the stopping motion of the bus.

"This where we get off. Ceel's apartment is nearby."

Naturally, Celia agreed to help. But she drew the line at letting a púca inside her apartment, so Jib and Brigit waited outside while the naiad collected items she felt might be helpful.

Brigit described Logan's current symptoms, as Celia locked the front door of her apartment and refreshed its protective seals. While they walked to the bus stop, Celia, who could use a cell phone, texted the wrestler to meet them at the apartment if he was available.

Finished, the naiad explained her theory to Brigit, "Logan's weakened condition may have made the effect of the Perilous more intense."

"No joke, Ceel," said Brigit. "That's why we need you. He looks pretty bad, and I don't think a human hospital would do him any good."

Her bondmate said, "How low to go behind your back and involve your parents."

Before Jib could speak, Brigit blurted out, "No worse than trying to kill me."

No one in Geheimetür knew who her parents were and Brigit planned on keeping it that way as long as possible. Behind Celia's back, she motioned to Jib by placing an index finger over her lips, begging his silence. The púca twitched its tail but said nothing.

While the three headed back on the bus, Celia continued talking, "I still think it was a pretty low thing to do."

"To be fair, I did laugh pretty hard when she trotted around the polo field neighing like a horse for two hours. It was hilarious."

Jib wanted to hear the story, so Brigit related it while they traveled back to the apartment.

Celia took Logan's temperature, pulse, and blood pressure while he slept through most of the exam. Celia showed the brownie the herbal tinctures she wanted Logan to drink.

"You're amazing," said Brigit, who thought it all a mystery. She wanted to believe in her friend's ability to help Logan.

"When humans return from the Perilous, it's not unusual for them to run a fever or feel tired afterward. However, Logan's immune system is probably weakened by the siren's Beguiling, making the situation serious. In the next twenty-four hours, we should see if he worsens or stabilizes. What he needs now is rest and plenty of fluids."

Granite arrived so Brigit, Jib, Celia, and the brownie met in the living room to discuss what to do. The dryad paced back and forth across the floor, telling the others, "We have to come up with a plan."

"A plan for -?" inquired Jib. The True Beast was lying across the back of the sofa, its eyes mostly closed. Whether in contentment, sleep, or thought, wasn't exactly clear.

"Logan won't be able to get to classes next week, but he can't afford to miss any more," explained Brigit. "He just got his grades back up."

"Grades?" asked the cat, causing Celia to whisper to it, "A measure of how well you are learning the material being taught."

Meanwhile, Granite gazed down at his large square hands to minutely examine his fingernails. He seemed uncomfortable as he mumbled, "I know a guy - "

When he paused and didn't continue, Brigit encouraged him to explain.

"This guy attends classes, especially ones that give credit for attendance. For people who can't attend. Subs in for them."

"No way," scoffed Brigit, returning to her pacing. "Logan's maestro would see through that Glamour in a second. Besides the school probably has some sort of protection against that."

"No, he wouldn't," insisted the wrestler. "This guy is a Doppelgänger."

"Oh, that might work!" Celia cried excitedly.

"Dangerous idea," said Jib, adding, "I like it."

Brigit stopped pacing and put her hand on her chin, to think over Granite's suggestion.

The Doppelgänger were mysterious beings. They were often recluses, with little to do with other fae. It wasn't known how their fae Glamour worked so they were viewed with suspicion.

Doppelgänger from the nine fairy courts had used their power to conceal the entire country of Bewachterberg. This work of magic was considered the gold standard of what the fae working together could achieve.

However, Doppelgänger serving as royal advisers was now out of fashion, and Brigit had never met one. She did know her parents found their magic disconcerting.

The dryad slowly said, "A Doppelgänger is more powerful than any of us. That puts us at a disadvantage in any negotiations. Do we want to be in Debt with one? Who knows what it might demand in payment."

Granite squirmed, his level of discomfort growing. However, he also didn't think it right Logan be punished for events out of his control.

"He helped a guy who wanted to skip town for the Oktoberfest up in Munich. But it worked for him. No one noticed that it wasn't him."

"A fetch be dangerous," said the brùnaidh. The others avoided making eye contact with her as doing so was considered rude by the Kindly Ones.

However, they all knew the brownie was right.

After another hour of discussing possible solutions, the group kept returning to using the Doppelgänger to cover for Logan's absence.

"Okay, line up a meeting, Granite," Brigit said, who was tired of discussing it. "We need him for two weeks, don't you think?"

Celia agreed that two weeks should do it. If not, they had a bigger problem. Granite interrupted the two fae women, "He takes only Bitcoin."

"What's that?" inquired Jib.

"It's a money exchange humans use to disguise who is paying whom," explained Brigit. She could see what the púca was about to suggest and she shook her head.

"No, Jib, you can't just turn leaves into gold and use it to pay a Doppelgänger. Thank goodness Logan has money so we can make it work somehow. But first, let's meet this Doppelgänger and find out what he can do, and for how much."

She handed Celia the school schedule of Logan's classes that the dryad had pulled from the fridge. Granite leaned over her shoulder to view it.

"For the first week, someone needs to be here to

162

help him eat, get to the bathroom, and make sure he's okay."

The True Beast was offended when the schedule they were planning didn't include it. "I'm fully capable of participating in this scheme."

Brigit sighed, saying, "Be practical. It's not like you can help him to the bathroom or make a hot toddy." At her comment, Jib jumped down and started to scratch the corner of the sofa. The dryad reprimanded the púca sharply, "Stop sulking."

However, no matter how the three naturals worked out the schedule, the brownie would need to cover most of the morning hours. Brigit felt guilty and uncertain about asking for her assistance.

"Lassie dinnae fatch yeself. Cooking, cleaning, and caring is in me blood."

Celia and Granite remained silent and left handling the brownie to Brigit. The Kindly Ones were easily offended when directly asked for assistance.

"Perhaps, but this kind of stuff isn't generally your province," said the dryad cautiously. "I know I'm not supposed to be grateful and all that but…"

"The laddie does leave a nice blend of cream and whiskey. Besides, how would I answer to me own liege if I left one of me own without assistance? The Great Queen would be right angry if I didn't lend a hand."

It took a few days to get an appointment with the Doppelgänger. The fae tried explaining it all to Logan, and maybe it was because he was still feeling unwell, but the American didn't understand how it was all to come together.

A being that could look like him? But wasn't a shapeshifter? How would anyone be fooled?

He decided not to worry about it and spent his days resting. Everything that happened in the Perilous Realm seemed like a dream until the black cat would sit on his pillow and start talking.

Today, though he was alone. Brigit and the others had run off to meet the Doppelgänger, leaving Logan to rest. Having had enough of being in bed, he wrapped up in a cocoon of blankets and settled in a chair on his balcony.

He was sipping a hot toddy prepared by Mrs. Tiggy when the crows came flying by. One landed on his balcony railing and asked if he had any more sunflower seeds to share. Reaching over to open a storage bucket, the college student grabbed a scoopful and tossed them onto the ground. Seeing the sudden bounty, two more crows landed, hopping over to chat with him.

"Not dead yet, huh?" the largest of the trio asked him, and Logan gave a smirk, "No. Not yet."

Since an incident in his childhood, Logan could speak with birds of the Corvid family. He had never met his grandmother's raven Mara again, but he always kept treats handy just in case.

The original speaker turned his head sideways to give Logan a speculative look. "Zitha, you've lost the betting pool." At the largest crow's comment, Zitha tucked his head under a wing, ashamed.

Logan inquired, "Betting pool?"

"Of course," said the leader of the crow's family group. "We've laid bets on when you'll keel over dead from the siren's spell. No hard feelings, I hope."

Logan had always considered the crows his friends, so it was a little unsettling that they didn't express any sympathy over his future demise.

"It might not happen. Have you considered that?" Logan challenged the birds.

"It'll happen," replied Zitha, who had recovered his equilibrium enough to grab some seeds.

"He looks pretty good today," croaked the smallest of the birds. She had given Logan the longest amount of days and was hoping to win big.

"Looks can be deceiving," warned their leader.

"Did no one bet I would survive?" asked Logan plaintively. When the trio stopped laughing, their senior replied with a firm, "No."

"Can I place a bet?" he said.

The crow hopped closer to Logan and cocked his head to give him another measuring stare. "You have to put something into the pot. Winner takes it all."

"What's the prizes so far?"

The other two, clearly younger and a bit more excitable, started hopping about in circles.

"Shiny coins! Pop-top lids! Gold chain! Aluminum foil!"

Logan fished in his pocket and brought out a shiny foil ball. It was a cat's toy he had insisted Brigit buy for Jib. He was hoping to show it to the púca, but the being had left with the others.

"We want that."

"Put it down."

"Let us see it."

Logan kept a hold of it, bringing it higher, so the red and silver foil caught the sun's rays. Not only did it make a pleasing crinkle sound, but its shiny surface fascinated the birds.

"It's yours if I can lay a bet," Logan suggested.

When the crows quickly agreed, he tossed the ping-pong-sized ball over to them. The two youngest argued over who was going to hold it, but their leader wasn't as easily distracted.

"What's your bet?" he asked.

"That I won't die."

The crows stopped playing soccer with the foil ball and blinked rapidly at Logan in astonishment.

"He's a bold one," said the smallest.

The crows huddled to decide. When they seemed to done discussing the matter, Logan spoke up before they could fly away.

"Wait. I want a different prize if I win."

"He doesn't want the buttons?"

"- the gold chain?"

"- and pop-tops?"

"Those sound irresistible," Logan said politely, "but I would rather win your service."

The crows clacked their beaks, but the crinkly ball of fun was too tempting. The smallest and boldest, asked, "What service would you want - if you were to win? Which in all fairness, I must say is very unlikely."

Thinking over Brigit's comments about the fae and his experiences in the Perilous Realm, Logan outlined his proposal.

"If I survive this semester, the three of you will stop by daily. Just to chat and share your gossip with me until I end my enrollment at LOTTOS."

The crows huddled again, cawing. It seemed they had agreed to Logan's proposal as the two youngest flew away, still arguing over who got to carry the toy back to their treasure stash. Their leader stayed behind outlining the revision to the agreement.

"You ask nothing but a share in what we know. That is a reasonable enough thing to give, especially as you are a descendant of our patroness. However, it is not enough that you live. To claim victory, not only must you survive, but your heart must be free of the siren by the end of the term."

With the deal sealed, he gave Logan a bob of farewell with his head before wheeling off into the sky after his fellows.

Chapter Fourteen
Double Trouble

The Doppelgänger sat at one of the study tables of the Leopold Otto central library. He found it amusing that whenever a fae desired his services, they requested a meeting at the library.

This library was part of the original monastery before it became a university in 1521. It was commonly believed that the wards within the building protected the students from magic. The fae being found this urban legend touching.

While the library's protections were robust, they were not enough to impair his abilities. But he did like the vaulted ceilings in the library. Very lovely. So it was worth the visit today to meet up with three fae who had requested his skills in solving an attendance problem.

Taking the place in class for fae students was interesting in many ways: he got to study subjects he usually wouldn't; was able to observe professors without their knowledge of his evaluations; and he learned a lot about what the fae student body was up to.

He watched the three fae approach. All were from the naturals Sept, and their magical elements were evident: the dryad was wood, the naiad was water, and the male eotan, stone. The spymaster had briefed himself before the meeting, so he was interested to see the faces behind the reports.

The dryad was short and wiry. She gave off an aura of cocky confidence. He had learned from his network of spies that while Brigit Cullen was canny, overall she was known as fair in her dealings. Though some thought she was perhaps a bit too rigid in adhering to the Laws of Civility.

He also knew that the dryad declined tangled commitments, which was unusual since more inexperienced freshmen stumbled in this area. For example, Cullen had spared the life of a low-ranking fae during a confrontation at the local beer hall last month. Most, would have simply killed the bog sprite.

That showed wisdom in one so young. The

anomaly intrigued him.

The second woman was an attractive, brown-haired naiad with an open face. Her clothes were an eclectic mix, bohemian but with French sophistication.

Like her bondmate, Celia Rivers was also known to be a careful person. Although considerate and friendly on the surface, she kept her distance in relationships. Professional. As a junior, she should have known not to meet one of his kind for any reason so it was a puzzle why she was here.

The most physically dangerous of the trio was the eotan wrestler due to his exceptional strength. Eotans were a wide range of beings encompassing savage trolls, hill dwarves, and mountain giants, and those who were very human-like such as Granite.

Granite Hillside was showing off a new beer stein, made from the head of a malevolent tulpa and he could respect what it would take to obtain such a trophy.

After nodding a greeting, the trio took a line of chairs opposite him at the library table. Brigit and Celia sat, while Granite stood behind them, his hands clasped in front of him.

The dryad placed a violin case she had been carrying on the study desk. She crossed her hands on the tabletop and waited as Granite introduced them all. The Doppelgänger gave a polite nod. As was typical among the fae, he gave a common name they could use to address him.

"Well, Paul," Brigit began, but she was interrupted by a black cat. The púca jumped onto the table and started to lick his back leg. The being had placed itself between Brigit and Paul, blocking their direct view.

With an aggrieved sigh, the dryad introduced it, "This is Jib."

The cat continued to bathe while asking the Doppelgänger, "Haunt or Harbinger? You're such rare, shy creatures I've never had the opportunity to ask."

Paul gave a closed-mouthed smile, saying, "Neither."

His response did not deter the chatty cat.

"Brigit, Celia, and Granite are all naturals. That's why they work so well together as bondmates. I'm a púca Trickster, affinity fire. But you know that already don't you?"

"Jib," Brigit muttered warningly, but being a True Beast, there was no restraining it. The cat's orange eyes madly flickered as it said, "Before doing deals, it's best to know who you are dealing with."

Paul gave the cat a nod and replied, "Since you feel so strongly about it, I'm a Mindbender."

At his words, Brigit's hand reached for the handle of the violin case, and she stood up. Her rising motion was copied by the naiad.

Paul raised his eyebrows.

"Does this bother you?"

Brigit was forthright.

"Of course it does. I mean, I knew your power would outrank us all, but this means you can convince us of anything. You could change our minds, without us even knowing. We couldn't trust that our judgment is our own."

He gently motioned with his hand for them to return to their seats.

"We are here to talk only. I have no bond which would influence me to hurt or persuade you. I swear this by the Laws of Civility. So let us discuss only possibilities before you are so quick to run away."

The trio looked at each other, and the fae women reluctantly sat back down. Paul folded his hands together on the table and began again.

"That's why my services are paid by human coin, not with favors," Paul reassured them. "Why don't you explain your request first?"

Brigit was still uncertain, so Granite began, "We three have an alliance."

"Which includes a human," clarified Celia.

"The human needs his classes attended, while he recovers from Fae Fever," explained Jib. The cat was still working its tongue along its leg.

The Doppelgänger raised his eyebrows, surprised. He had never been approached by the fae to help a human. His mandate had limits. Paul said, apologetically, "I only sub for the fae, not humans."

The trio exchanged glances again but did not move to leave. Brigit cleared her throat, her tone sharp.

"We wouldn't be here if the university would do its job. Students come here and think they are safe. But how safe can it be when humans are in danger from the fae the university refuses to rein in?"

The perceived injustice seemed to be a favorite hobby-horse of the dryad. Her voice gained volume, "Nothing disgusts me more than those who enjoy the benefits of authority, but don't take seriously the responsibility of their duties."

There was a short, awkward silence before the púca added, in a relaxed purring voice, "The human is Beguiled by a siren student, name of Sibyl. Do you know her?"

Paul said nothing, but what the Trickster revealed interested him. He knew the siren had ensnared Franco Sabbatini, but not another human. After the dramatic loss of the polo team at their last match, Paul had been ordered by his liege to investigate the troublesome siren. Being love-Beguiled, Sabbatini had played a sloppy and disgraceful game.

The cat continued, his purr growing louder.

"It's my understanding, and of course I've only been in Bewachterberg for a day, so perhaps I am wrong, but isn't a fae threatening the life of a human student considered a violation of the Treaty?"

At Jib's comment, the dryad appeared excited.

"The Treaty of Sigismund could be our solution."

The Doppelgänger quickly dashed her hope.

"Not exactly," said Paul, lacing his fingers and bringing them to his chin. He explained. "The Treaty is very clear that fae upon fae actions are under the jurisdiction of the royal fae kingdoms the beings owe allegiance to. Since it is the nature of the fae to play tricks upon humans, we are allowed some latitude."

"You talk like a law student who puts theory above beings," snapped Brigit.

"Law is one of my areas of study," Paul admitted, giving another close-mouthed smile.

"But what if it involves a life?" interrupted Celia.

"At that point, the situation becomes problematic."

Celia turned to Brigit, saying, "We should bring this up to the Rector."

Granite leaned over between them and said, "That's what I told Logan, but he doesn't feel a human could do anything against one of our kind."

Brigit drummed her fingers on the table, thinking. "As a law student, would you bring this to the Chancellor's attention?"

The Mindbender suspended time while he thought over their problem.

LOTTOS was under the administrative guidance of a Rector and a Chancellor. The Rector was in charge of almost everything concerning the management of the student body and the administration of classes and professors. This position was traditionally held by a human, as it was now.

The second position was traditionally held by a fae from Bewachterberg's royal line. The Chancellor was a ceremonial position for pomp and circumstance. He was trotted out for the dog-and-pony show of graduation, ribbon cuttings, fundraising, and to meet Bewachterberg royalty.

The spymaster worked directly for the Chancellor. His warrant was to keep an eye on the fae, to make sure bodies stayed buried, and those who needed to forget what they saw, did so.

It was true he had never assisted a human before. However, the Mindbender wasn't personally against the idea. It might even be entertaining. Far more entertaining than sitting in a boring physics lecture about light cones and their relationship to absolute future and absolute past.

However, in helping a human, did he fulfill his mandate from his liege?

The spymaster's primary purpose on the campus was to glean information about what the fae students were up to and pass it along to the Chancellor who would decide if further action was needed.

For example, a harmless desire by a student to skip

class to waste time was trivial. Asking a Doppelgänger to take tests to complete a degree was another.

After re-starting time, he suggested the fae beings give him the details. Brigit pulled out a folded piece of paper from her pocket, sliding it over to him.

"This is Logan's schedule. He needs these classes attended for at least two weeks until spring break."

Paul glanced over the schedule. It was doable, and if he needed to, he would bend time to be at two places at once.

"And this instrument," Paul gestured to the case, "figures into this human's class load?"

"He's in the orchestra," explained the dryad, "Can you play the violin?"

"I don't need to play," the Mindbender explained. "Human or fae will see what they expect to see. Hear what they expect to hear."

The cat had finished its bath and was now lying, paws tucked, in a loaf position, its eyes closed to the smallest slits.

"So it's true that your element is Time and Memory?" Jib said.

Shocked, the two fae women stood up again to leave.

Jib sat in that immobile attitude of a cat who meant business. It suggested, "Why don't you let him look at the violin? He'll find it interesting, I'm sure."

Brigit reluctantly turned back. She replaced the

case of the musical instrument on the table, shoving Jib's sprawling form further down the length of the surface.

"It's Logan's instrument. Since you just stated you won't require it to convince anyone, I don't see why you need to see it."

"Show it to him," insisted Jib, and Brigit reluctantly unsnapped the case, lifting the lid to expose its contents. The violin lay nestled in its green velvet-lined container, the wood of the instrument glowing warmly. Paul bent over it and gave an audible, indrawn hiss.

"This is the human's instrument? How long has he owned it? How did he obtain it? Who gave it to him? When?"

"Why? Is it valuable?" asked Celia.

Brigit bit her lip, trying to remember Logan's words, "He said it was a gift from his grandmother. I know there's a protection on it but…"

"Oh, there's a protection on it all right," agreed Paul, as he sketched a complicated movement with his hand. A trail of fire visible only to their small group shot to the height of the cathedral ceiling.

"Who exactly is Logan's grandmother?" demanded Paul. "Because this complicates things exceedingly."

The cat smiled.

"Oh, I think once the Morrighan finds out her grandson is under the thrall of a siren and likely to die before the semester ends, Bewachterberg might find itself in the middle of a war, don't you?" purred the cat.

Chapter Fifteen
Coffee Talk

Paul, the Doppelgänger, entered the Chancellor's outer office. As with most of his interactions with humans, the secretary saw the person she expected.

"Guten Tag, Professor Schneider. You're early for your appointment. Let me see if the Chancellor's ready to receive you."

The woman picked up her phone, making a quick call to the inner office. Receiving permission, she gestured him to pass through. Paul gave a polite knock on the heavily carved door of the Chancellor's office before going in.

He found the Chancellor standing in front of a

marble fireplace winding a clock. François Auguste Bandemer swore at the instrument in colorful French before thrusting it back on the mantle in impatience.

"Damn thing hasn't kept the right time since 1815." Turning, he saw his spymaster. "Frau Hofmann said it was that Schneider, coming again to complain about how small his office is. Imagine that! Look about you at this shoebox I'm stuck within. But do I complain?"

Since the Chancellor's office was quite spacious, with it an en suite attached to a public area containing two large desks, a conference table, as well as two sofas, Paul said nothing in reply. He had decades to learn how to handle Bandemer, and part of it was knowing when to keep quiet.

The fae king was still wearing his winter ensemble as prescribed by the wardrobe policies outlined by Louis XIV. He wore a velvet coat of deep purple over an off white satin waistcoat embroidered with colorful fall leaves and fastened with silver buttons. His cream satin breeches came to right below his knees where a red garter kept his silk stockings in place. The ribbons matched the red heels of his leather shoes.

This was the Chancellor's casual wear. Since May was a full month away, the fae king was still wearing his *hiver* wardrobe.

The Mindbender bowed to his liege and said, "Something has occurred that needs your immediate attention."

While Paul related his recent encounter with the fae students and the violin, the Chancellor toyed at the layers of lace under his chin. The froth of expensive lace was held in place by a ruby pin. As large as a man's thumb, the gemstone looked like a spot of blood amongst the snow.

"Logan Dannon? I don't recall the name. Have you checked his pedigree?"

"I did. The student is from an American family."

The Chancellor gave a negligent wave upon hearing the information. Americans were of little interest to him despite the Rector's insistence on increasing their enrollment. While the Rector felt paying students could offset the free tuition given to the fae, the Chancellor didn't care about the nuts and bolts of the university's operation.

"Expel him," Bandemer said. "Send him back home to die from the siren's Beguiling. If he expires on his home soil, he won't be our problem."

While this method had worked for other students who had run afoul of the various fae, Paul explained why expulsion would not solve this particular problem.

"The family seems to be closely tied to a deity. The fae I met said the violin was a gift from his grandmother. However, the protection has the signature of the Celtic goddess, the Morrighan."

The Chancellor threw the stapler across the room.

Paul didn't flinch. The Chancellor's reaction was not unexpected, and his liege was not unknown for his hot temper, as dents in the wood paneling could testify.

The fae did not involve themselves with gods and goddesses for good reason. While the fae did not consider humans on the same level as themselves, deities were powerful and fickle. Involvement with them often resulted in the loss of property and lives.

When Bandemer's temper returned to a low boil, Paul inquired, "How would you like me to proceed?"

The Chancellor pinched his bony nose, squeezing his eyes shut.

"Find out more. Who is this boy? Where did he come from? How far along is he from wasting away?"

The Chancellor opened his light blue eyes the color of glacier chips.

"That siren already cost me a match against our rival. Now, the prince of Bewachterberg is arriving in a few short weeks for our festivities. I cannot and will not have things about here in shambles. I don't care if we expel the lot of them. I will have my parade!"

"That was weird even by fae standards," said Celia.

Granite denied any responsibility, "Hey, I just heard about him from a buddy. Don't blame me for how bizarre he is. If I'd known he was a Mindbender I'd never have suggested a meeting."

Brigit said, "Weird or not, at least he's agreed to help."

They had returned in one piece from their meeting with the Doppelgänger, and Brigit opened Logan's bedroom door slowly and peeked in. Seeing he was awake, she entered and started to tell him their mission had been successful.

"This Paul character will attend all your classes and keep us updated about assignments. He thinks it likely any tests will take place right after spring break since professors love to drop a test right after a holiday. That gives you about three weeks before you have to get to classes by yourself."

"That sounds good," said Logan, "but why do you look upset?"

"Well, it turns out that Doppelgänger are, surprise, surprise, Mindbenders."

"You've lost me."

Celia followed Brigit into the room, bringing a glass of water with some pills for Logan's fever. She helped him up, placing pillows expertly behind him while Brigit continued.

"All fae have a power affiliation to an element. We recognize seven: wood, metal, stone, water, wind, flame, and the last is a blend of powers - time/memory. For example, since I'm a dryad, mine is wood; Celia's is water; and stone for Granite."

"That makes sense."

"Well, you can't always predict it by Sept," Bridget explained. "The brownie would most likely be metal but she could be stone, water, or flame."

"What's Jib?"

At this name, Jib landed in the middle of Logan's stomach. Seeing the cat's eyes, Logan guessed, "Flame?" as the púca started to knead a cozy spot in the blankets.

"Right, but púcas can also be water, like a kelpie. I had thought Doppelgänger simply used Glamor but it turns out they use the most dangerous and powerful element of all: time and memory. Mindbenders can distort things. They have the ability to change timelines and implant memories of things that never happened."

Sitting at the end of his bed, Celia chimed in, "It was thought the Doppelgänger hid Bewachterberg from the world for 99 years and a day with Glamour. But I guess not. It must have been Mindbending."

Jib interrupted. "Tell it, Brigit. Tell how the fae took a country and hid it from the world. It's one of my favorite bedtime stories."

Brigit smiled at the cat, giving it a stroke from ears to tail, before beginning her narrative.

"In 1891, the King of Bewachterberg consulted a Cassandra about the welfare of his country's future. A

Cassandra is one powerful in prophecy."

Logan nodded his head, thinking of his cousin, Evie.

"He was told Bewachterberg was heading towards a turbulent time. Worse than the Thirty Years War. Not only would Bewachterberg suffer from two world wars but it would be absorbed and divided, losing its sovereignty. It would eventually come under Russian control. This true vision of his country's future horrified him for like all good kings he was devoted to the welfare of his people."

In the middle of the story, Granite arrived. He leaned against the doorway, eating a warm piece of cake the brownie had just made.

"But the Cassandra told him all was not lost. The king could ensure Bewachterberg would escape such a dire fate if he made an agreement with the fae. If the king would pledge himself to nine fae queens and acknowledge their children as his heirs, the nine courts would unite to protect Bewachterberg for 99 years and a day."

"The king agreed, but he was no fool. He knew the fae's real desire was to gain control of his country through his descendants. After the pledging ceremony, he abdicated the throne. So while his offspring would never rule, they did inherit his wealth and status."

"So that is why the royal family of Bewachterberg is merely a figurehead," said Celia.

"But if he tricked them," asked the American, "why did the fae help Bewachterberg at all?"

"That was the contract, Logan," explained Brigit patiently. "Contracts can have loopholes, but the essentials can't be changed. His descendants were still his recognized heirs. In the end, the nine courts wouldn't rule Bewachterberg, but they could have a home in the human lands."

Granite said around the last bit of his cake, "I never knew how the courts worked it. But it makes perfect sense knowing the Doppelgänger are Mindbenders."

Over the next two decades, the Perilous removed the knowledge of Bewachterberg from the world. Mindbenders, the court wizards, worked to warp time and memory, causing the country to disappear from maps.

People forgot they had traveled there, and when they came to a road that would enter Bewachterberg, they would turn aside and go another direction. Within thirty years, Bewachterberg had become nothing but a fabled land as much as Atlantis was.

Under Jib's purring warmth, Logan's eyes started to close, and his mind softened with sleep, under Brigit's voice.

"The contract ended in 1989, the year the Berlin wall fell. Suddenly, Bewachterberg emerged from her long dream, like a sleeping beauty."

Brigit tried to dissuade Logan from meeting Paul, but to her frustration, the human insisted. However, she put her foot down on allowing the Doppelgänger entrance to the apartment.

Upon her insistence, Logan was sitting at a table in a local bakery, barely able to hold himself upright, drinking a glass of orange juice when the Doppelgänger sat down across from him.

Logan startled and the Paul asked in a deep voice that was smooth and neutral, "What do you see, bard?"

"The most dangerous fae I've encountered yet."

The fae had a sideways smile as if he had just heard a hidden joke and countered, "I see a very sick human who should be in bed."

"That's accurate, I suppose."

The college student put the glass down, his hand shaking from fatigue. Behind the Doppelgänger's head, he could see Brigit, a worried frown on her face. She was seated at another table close by, but the blueberry muffin in front of her remained untouched.

"So the rumor appears to be correct," said Paul. "Bards see my true form."

"Well, maybe. Sibyl taught me that I don't see as clearly as I believed."

"When it comes to love, every man has adjusted

their reality to fit what they desire. There is grounds for believing love is blind."

Logan's mouth was dry so he took another sip of orange juice.

"Perhaps," the college student said, "but I didn't come here to talk about my love life."

The Doppelgänger gave him a nod and opened his hand, palm up, showing it empty as an encouragement for Logan to continue. The American gave a little cough to clear his throat and began, "Having you attend classes in my place doesn't seem fair to me. I've agreed to Brigit's plan out of desperation. But all the homework and tests I will do myself. I will also go to the orchestra rehearsals. It's not fair to the maestro to get a look-alike who won't play."

"I won't complain," agreed the Mindbender. "Less work for me. But, if you don't mind my saying so, you don't look like you could lift a violin."

"I'll lift my violin, and I will play it." Logan's jaw jutted forward in a way very familiar to his parents.

Paul took a sip of his coffee, the mug hiding a smile.

"Speaking of violins, I saw yours. It's a beautiful instrument."

Logan replied, looking down at the table, "It's not a Stradivarius or anything like that. Or magic. It's an ordinary violin."

"I am curious to know where you got it."

"From my grandmother. She always wanted my father to pursue a musical career. When she heard I was in the orchestra she gave it to me on my twelfth birthday."

"When you speak of your grandmother, is this an honorary position or blood connection?"

Ah, so he knew. Logan sighed. He guessed his secret couldn't remain secret where the fae were involved.

"It's a blood connection. I'm a direct descendant."

Paul always made sure statements were accurate so he asked again for clarification.

"So you're a grandson of the goddess, the Morrighan?"

"Yes."

The two sat quietly, the hum of the bakery customers around them, making the moment ordinary. The rich smell of roasting coffee beans permeated the air.

"I understand you have a problem with a certain siren here at LOTTOS. Have you thought to contact the Great Queen about the matter?"

Logan gave a bitter smile born from experience.

"Asking my granny to intervene often leads to events best not experienced. Because of her, my mother thought she was a zombie for awhile, and I got lost on a mountain."

Paul took another sip of his coffee while Logan

toyed with his now empty glass. The silence was not uncomfortable, rather it was contemplative as both pursued their thoughts. Finally, the fae said, "You are an interesting human. I will help you attend classes until your Fae Fever is resolved. However, I prefer to do it for a favor to be redeemed later."

"Favor?" asked Logan alarmed. "Brigit said you accepted human money? I'm not sure I want to commit to some vague favor to be redeemed at some indefinite date in the future. That sounds like a horrible idea."

The Mindbender gave another sideways smile. It made him appear human, which he certainly was not.

"Someone has been teaching you about our ways. Would that be the dryad? I hear the two of you have a Debt?"

Logan sat up straighter, the stubborn brace of his jaw returning.

"Leave Brigit out of this."

"Calm down, my young cockerel, I have no intention of inflicting harm to you or your bondmates. I find your situation intriguing enough on its own. Since you will be doing the classwork, it leaves me little to do. All I ask is an audience with the Morrighan if the possibility presents itself."

Logan thought it over.

"As long as this agreement does not put me or mine in harm's way or obligates us to a course of action, I will agree to it. On the understanding that I only provide the opportunity for a meeting. I do not stand for how my grandmother would react to it."

The two shook hands. Because Logan did love truth and thought the Doppelgänger should understand what he just promised, he added, "If you meet, and your motivation is to harm her, she will take care of you."

"I'm sure Badb Catha, the Battle Crow and Great Queen, would pound me into raw hamburger," said the spymaster.

Business concluded, Paul stood up. Passing Brigit, the Doppelgänger told her, "We need to talk, later. Privately."

Chapter Sixteen
Stormy Weather

ranite was sitting in the auditorium waiting for Logan to finish his rehearsal. He didn't know much about music but it looked like they were done as some of the musicians were standing and others were packing away their instruments.

Celia slid into the seat next to him, whispering, "I thought I was supposed to take the human home today?"

"Coach didn't have any worthy opponents for me," explained the wrestler, giving a shrug. "Sent me off early. Thought I'd stop by here and see if you and Logan wanted to grab lunch."

Celia pulled a small package of candies from her purse and offered the open bag to the wrestler. He pulled a few out, while she said, "We've got a problem. I saw Sybil hanging around in the lobby. I think she's here for Logan."

"Hm," said Granite, sucking hard on the sour candy. "I really don't like her. Do you?"

"Absolutely do not like her."

The two sat back watching the stage. When Logan looked up, Celia waved to him, receiving a nod in return.

Finished with his candy, Granite said, "Sybil's obsession with Logan all seems a bit much, don't you think? It borders on what humans call a vendetta. Why not release him? She had her fun."

"Some girls just can't let go," replied Celia. "They can't stand the thought their place in a guy's heart would be supplanted by someone else."

"That doesn't make any sense," Granite frowned. "She's already moved on. Why fixate on an ex?"

"I can't tell you for sure, Granite, but it seems to be a trophy thing based around an ego trip. Like they take pride in their list of conquests. And in the fact that no one can replace them. Like a child who if she's told to share a toy, breaks it."

Granite grunted as he stood up. "I still think it is excessive. If Logan had wronged her, or if he had a bondmate that had insulted her, of course I could see

Sybil's reasoning. But hanging around, stalking him? Trying to kill Brigit because she's his roommate? That's twisted."

Celia shrugged. "She does seem a bit histrionic."

Logan had reached them. Climbing up the stairs had him slightly out of breath as he greeted them.

"Hey Celia, Granite, I didn't know you were both coming. Did you get to hear any of the practice? It's really coming together I think."

Before either one of the fae could reply, Sybil entered through the auditorium doors, putting a damper on the group.

"Hello, sweetie. I see you have two watchdogs with you today. Where's that tree hugger? She's usually following you around like a faithful dog."

Granite stepped between her and Logan, stone forcing wind to change direction. Sibyl's spell flowed around them, drifting away.

The siren narrowed her eyes.

"When did you become a bondmate with a human?"

Granite chuckled. Mountains didn't intimidate easily.

"Maybe because your network isn't well developed or you're stunted in your brain that you don't get how all this works. Brigit's like a little sister. Met her when she fell out of an oak tree. Helped her get enrolled at LOTTOS. Showed her the ropes. If she owes this human a Debt, I owe him one too."

Celia moved so she was shoulder to shoulder with Granite, blocking Sibyl's view of Logan. "When you enrolled at LOTTOS you agreed to a contract. I find it personally insulting how you've ignored it."

The blond siren sneered at the naiad. "Go wet yourself. The fae run this place and if anyone had a problem with what I've done they would have stopped me by now."

"We are stopping you," rumbled Granite.

From behind them, Logan said, in an attempt to get the fae's attention, "Guys, can we stop this, please. Okay?"

For as the three beings talked, the manifestation of their affiliation's powers had increased. The ground under their feet had started to tremble. A pelting rain was hitting the auditorium's roof so hard it sounded like hail and the resulting noise was deafening. All four sets of the auditorium doors had blown open, hitting the walls hard, as a wind chased down the aisles, turning over music stands, and blowing papers across the stage.

No one paid attention to Logan but when Kados Géza, the university's conductor, slammed his open palm down on his stand, the confrontation stopped.

"Conduct yourselves with decorum when you are in my auditorium. Get out and play your fae games elsewhere!"

Shamefaced, the four shuffled out in a line, with Sibyl flouncing in the lead. In the lobby, Celia called out to her as she was exiting the front door, "I'd recommend not drinking any water in the next 24 hours. It might not sit well with you."

Sibyl shot her a glare before leaving. In a moment, they heard a small scream of pain.

"Too bad she tripped on that sidewalk. Now where do we want to go for lunch?" said Granite.

A few days later when Logan was bent over a textbook trying to read the same sentence for the fifth time, Brigit gave a slight cough. He looked over to where she was curled up on the other end of the sofa.

The dryad was surrounded by square pillows of green and yellow. Once was placed in front of her belly, her arms wrapped around it. The pillows were only one of the many changes he had noticed since she started living in his apartment. Other alterations were a floor rug in the living room and a bunch of plants in colorful pots positioned near the windowsill. All the white dishware in the kitchen had become blue, red, and green.

Brigit had certainly put her stamp on things around the place. But Logan didn't complain. The place felt more comfortable and besides, somehow she even removed the green stain from the tulpa out of his

199

bedroom carpet.

She was staring at him while twirling something flat and silver between her fingers. It took him a moment to recognize it as the leaf he had picked up in the Perilous Realm.

"You didn't pluck this off one of my trees, did you?" Brigit's tone was neutral even though her words were not.

Since his return, the fae hadn't asked Logan what happened when he was in the PR. There never seemed to be the time to discuss it so he now explained about the contest with her father.

She was frowning with displeasure by the end of the story but her ire was not directed at him.

"He's always interfering with my life! Goes on about his kingly dignity and how any bondmate of mine becomes a bondmate of his. How I need to choose my friends carefully or I could dishonor him. So irritating. It's one of the reasons I haven't told anyone here about my family."

"Don't worry," Logan reassured her. "I haven't told anyone the details of what happened."

Brigit reached over and placed the leaf on a cushion that lay between them. She said softly, "The grove gave you this as a gift."

Logan didn't pick it up, saying instead, "I think they gave it to me to pass on to you."

His words must have touched her as Brigit's eyes

watered before she looked away to stare at a blank wall.

"I think they miss you. Keep it. You'll be back one day."

Her fingers trembled slightly as they retrieved the leaf, tucking it under her shirt next to her skin. Logan didn't comment upon it but instead went back to reading his textbook with a slight smile.

Over the next few weeks of his recovery, Celia, Granite, and Jib were given official permission to enter Logan's apartment so he came to know them all in different ways.

Celia had a cool sophistication that was a little daunting, rather like an older sister who was the first to date. Seeing the dangerous side of her water affiliation during the confrontation with Sibyl had made him a little wary. So he cautiously asked Celia what type of debt he would owe her for helping him.

"Don't worry about it. You owe me nothing. I'm doing this because I can't stand what Sibyl is doing to our reputation," she explained to Logan one afternoon.

"Her fae mischief makes us all look bad. Her actions, if we don't stop her, are going to have longterm repercussions."

In the last few weeks, as promised, Paul had attended classes while Logan did all the homework. The college student had dragged himself to a philosophy class to take one test, and he had attended every one of his rehearsals even though Kados Géza was critical of his playing.

During those weeks, he had more time to hang with the wrestler. Perhaps because they were both males, Granite was the most open about himself, his family, and his connection with Brigit.

"I helped her get enrolled when she first arrived in Geheimetur. Now, she's tutoring me in math. It all evens out."

Boom-Boom made a green protein smoothie as he talked. The mess the wrestler was making in the kitchen alarmed Logan. He did not want his brownie angered to the point of becoming a boggart so he went behind Granite, washing out the blender and wiping down the kitchen counter and backsplash.

"Besides, now that the Doppelgänger is done subbing for you, he could call in your debt anytime. I feel guilty about getting you involved with him."

"It's fine," Logan reassured him.

Finished with his smoothie, Granite put his glass in the sink. Logan rinsed it out before setting it on the drainboard as the wrestler wandered out of the kitchen to the living room.

He called back over his shoulder, "Can you keep

count for me? Today's my light day, but I still need to get a workout done."

Granite explained each exercise as he went through his demanding sequence: "The wide-grip push-up engages the shoulders more. That's important for my wrestling. When I move my elbows and hands in closer, that works the triceps. I guess my personal favorite would have to be the clap push-up."

From a clap in front of his chest, he changed to a clap behind his back, pushing his chest off the ground.

"That's a Muay Thai push-up."

"Fascinating," yowled the black cat. The púca had found a sunbeam and was stretched out upon the windowsill to enjoy it.

After a series of walking jump push-ups, Granite bounded to his feet and without a pause, started his lower body routine, as he asked, "So what type of bird was Sibyl?"

"I don't know."

"Big mistake, Logan. You can't discount the beast-side of a shapeshifter. It's essential to their nature. Bird types especially. For example, my mom's a harpy, and her vulture side is pretty strong. She can't resist constantly pecking over dead subjects."

Squats became jumping squats.

"I'd bet she's something predatory. Ever hear of the

Butcherbird? It impales its victim."

Not wanting to hear more, Logan decided to change the subject. "Where is everyone this morning? Brigit left early. Is she working today?"

Jib meowed, "Royalty in town. Some noisy parade. Everyone is rushing about."

"The Bewachterberg prince is here," said Granite, while stretching. "Someone from the royal family comes for commencement. Celia is working at the First Aid tent. Brigit's boss is supplying plants for the parade floats. It's a big event for Geheimetür. "

The cat appeared only interested in licking a paw, but its fiery eyes and twitching tail indicated tension as it told Logan, "Brigit is meeting the human prince. She plans to trade him to the siren in order to free your heart."

"What!?"

Granite yelled, "Jib! you weren't supposed to tell him!"

The True Beast ignored the eotan's outrage. Examining its paw with narrowed eyes, the cat asked Logan, "What are you going to do about that, human?"

Chapter Seventeen
Secret Decoder Ring

The parade was forming at the parking lot near the tennis courts. Despite the crowd, finding the location of the prince of Bewachterberg wasn't difficult. It was where all the screaming girls were being held back by security.

Brigit squeezed through, until she found herself standing beside the Sibyl. The fae did not acknowledge the dryad's appearance.

Looking the same direction as the Sibyl, Brigit saw the prince of Bewachterberg. The handsome human was in his mid-twenties, wearing a long-sleeved, open-collared dress shirt in a deep wine color and dress slacks of deep navy blue. His leather belt showed off his flat stomach and slim hips.

An honorary sash in the colors of the Bewachterberg flag draped across his chest from shoulder to opposite hip.

Brigit had to admit, the prince of Bewachterberg was a fine-looking human. She figured he'd be someone her mother would have labeled a rake, a Casanova, and one delicious morsel.

In contrast, standing next to him was an ancient fae elf of vast power. From his aura and outfit, Brigit figured he was the Chancellor. Who else would be wearing an *été* outfit from 17th century France?

Her mother would have loved his clothes. His silk frock coat had an ombré effect of silver to purple, and was worn over a vest embroidered with flowers and butterflies. There was so much lace at throat and cuffs, you couldn't see his neck or hands. One hand played with opening and closing a fan.

Probably impatient for the parade to begin, as Brigit didn't think he was the nervous type.

"Going to be hard to get your hooks in him with all the security around."

"Guards will not stop me," the siren said loftily. The dryad laughed.

"I guess you didn't notice his entourage are a bunch of half-bloods? And the humans are all wearing iron. Oh, and how will you bypass the Chancellor, who looks like he could take out a battalion of fae, let alone one bird-brain blond?"

"Shut up, Brigit. I'm not asking for your advice."

"Oh, you're not? Okay."

A security guard was doing a sweep, coming down their line and Brigit called out to him. What probably made him pause was that the dryad was reaching over the barricade and held out between her fingers a heavy man's ring.

The dryad took advantage of the man's hesitation and shouted, "Your prince will recognize this," as she tossed the ring his direction.

The guard instinctively caught it. He looked at it for a moment then back to Brigit before walking to where the prince stood.

"Where'd you get that ring?" the siren demanded suspiciously.

"In the library is a case full of old artifacts. They all have historical significance to the Bewachterberg royal family. I broke the lock last night and stole it."

Before Sibyl could help herself, the siren muttered, "I wish I'd thought of that."

"But you didn't," pointed out Brigit.

The two fae women watched as the guard showed the ring to the prince and gestured back to Brigit. The prince and the dryad made eye contact. After more conversation, the guard returned to where Brigit stood.

"Come along, fae. He'll hear your petition."

Brigit put her butt on top of the barricade and swung her legs over.

"See ya, later, Sibyl."

Sibyl watched in disbelief as Brigit walked right up to the prince of Bewachterberg. The royal even stepped away from the Chancellor to be private with the dryad!

The two were talking, but between the noise and distance, the siren wasn't able to understand what was being said. Seeing a pigeon flying overhead, Sibyl seized it with her magic. She forced the bird to land near the prince and Brigit. As the bird pecked at their feet, the siren eavesdropped.

"The ring provides one boon, but only one," the prince was saying. "Are you sure you want to use it for this?"

The prince's voice was cultured, giving Sibyl a thrill. She was so close to attaining her heart's desire! So close. If she captivated him, her queen would reward her well. If she could complete this mission, she'd have the status and admiration she had always craved from her home court.

Through the bird, she heard Brigit's reply of, "Yes, your highness."

"This afternoon then. After the parade, just show the ring to the guards, and they'll let you come up to my room."

Brigit waited politely as the prince walked back to the Chancellor. The two climbed into the back seat of a convertible and the decorated car took its place in line.

The crowd was cheering the prince's departing vehicle, as Sibyl pushed them out of her way to pursue Brigit. Emerging from the press of people, she saw the dryad ahead of her, walking back toward the quad.

Using the wind to speed along, the siren was able to catch up to her.

"You planned that," Sibyl accused her. "You don't want the prince. I do. You know that."

"Yep," Brigit kept walking. Her disregard made Sibyl seethe.

"And the price for the ring is Logan, I suppose."

"See," said Brigit, brightly, shaking her pointer finger at the blond, "I knew you'd be able to connect the dots. You're not as stupid as you look."

As protocol dictated, the two kept a distance from each other. It made holding a conversation rather tricky since Brigit kept putting trees between her and the siren.

"How do I know it isn't a fake? That all this isn't a setup?"

Brigit stopped walking and turned to face Sibyl.

"Sure, whatever. I promise you on the Laws of Civility that this ring will get you a meeting. I think that's worth the heart of a human you don't care about."

Sibyl licked her dry lips. Her eyes went to the ring Brigit held. When she said nothing, Brigit said impatiently, "Stop your clucking and get to making the deal. Release Logan from your spell. Promise you will not contact him again or attempt to Beguile him in any way, shape, or form."

"You do love your Laws of Civility don't you?"

"Yes, I do, as should you. Don't play by the rules, don't get the ring. Means you don't get the prince. Got it?"

"Well-played, dryad."

Neither had moved. As the two fae had been talking, the intensity of their moods brought a bit of the Perilous into the human lands. It formed a bubble around them, hiding them from the view of passers-by. Within it, the air grew darker, and the wind strong until it was snarling at their hair, tearing at their clothes.

The branches of the trees over their heads whipped back and forth. Fallen leaves swirled in a whirlwind around the two fae.

"I guarantee the ring gets you a meeting," Brigit promised again. "After that what you can achieve is up to you. Personally, I'd advise you pass on the ring and forget the prince. But you seem to have a rather narrow view of things."

"I'm not here to listen to your opinions, Brigit Cullen."

Brigit leaned her back against the big tree behind her. She crossed her arms and waited. The siren spoke first.

"I want him. I want the prince."

"Yeah, I get that. It's the why I don't understand," said Brigit, puzzled. "I mean, he's good looking and everything, but so are a lot of guys. Is it because he's a prince or what?"

"He's descended from the human king that tricked our courts," explained Sibyl. "My queen loathes his family line. If I Beguile the prince, I know it will earn me a seat at my queen's high table."

Brigit sighed. Was all this because Sibyl was chasing glory?

"This isn't the king who made the Treaty of Sigismund. That guy is long gone. I know time flows differently in the Perilous Realm —."

Sibyl interrupted her.

"I know that. In my court, what his ancestor did 100 human years ago is talked about as if it was yesterday. Our queen remembers the contract she signed. Being forced to protect Bewachterberg without the reward of her child ruling it."

The fae were known for holding grudges. They

remembered ancient insults as if they occurred yesterday. It was another reason Brigit had left; being tormented for a hundred years because she put a frog down someone's back when she was seven wasn't for her.

"Fair enough," said the dryad. "But why Beguile Logan? I mean he's just a nobody. Just another ordinary human college student."

Sibyl laughed, flashing pointed canines.

"When I saw Logan in line, getting his registration finalized, I could smell the hope on him. That optimistic yearning where everything is possible. It went straight to my head. When I discovered he was a bard, how could I resist the challenge he presented? Telling him enough of the truth that he believed everything I said without giving away my end game of destroying him."

At the expression on Brigit's face, the siren added, "You've never had a man in your power before? A man so helplessly in love he would do anything for you? Crushing their hopes and dreams is so delicious."

The siren shifted to her natural form. Her face and torso remained human but from the top of her head sprouted plumage composed of blue feathers. From her shoulders hung wings in shades of of brown and black. While down her back fell a long cascade of peacock feathers, making a colorful blue and green feathered train.

Like many fae shapeshifters, her feet showed her beast side: they ended in a three-toed bird claw with a sharp spur behind.

"So all you ask is I let Logan go? But what of Franco? Or anyone else I might have Beguiled while in Geheimetür?"

"I don't care about the other humans. Logan is my bondmate. Getting him free fulfills my Debt."

This type of thinking was fae, and Sibyl completely understood Brigit. The fae weren't altruistic.

"See you are no different than I."

"I'm totally different than you."

Sibyl's mocking laugh was the haunting shriek of a peacock.

"Don't fool yourself, my dear. What of the Fiat between us?"

"That's separate. But I'll put it aside for another day."

The siren advanced towards the dryad, and Brigit faded into the tree. The dryad's nature allowed her to inhabit any tree. But since this particular oak did not contain the Perilous and wasn't a portal, the siren could not follow.

The dryad's voice floated through the air, "Promise, Sibyl. I'll come out and play when you agree to my contract."

"Come out," the siren called to her, "It's a deal."

Brigit emerged from a different tree, causing Sibyl

to spin around to face her.

"Formally now. Agree to my terms."

Sibyl ground her teeth before replying.

"I agree. Logan will be released when I hold the ring. I will not harm him or anything he considers his once I have the ring. The ring only gives me a meeting. I understand there are no more promises attached to it."

The siren lunged forward, but the dryad faded out again, merging her essence into a great oak.

"Now, now, bird-brain, play fair," Brigit cautioned her adversary. "Why would I give the ring before you release Logan?"

"By the same thinking, why would I trust you, knothead?"

Again, Brigit emerged from a tree different than the one she had entered. She had leaves in her hair and her brown skin held an undertone of green.

"Because I'm trustworthy and you aren't?"

"I swore. Isn't that enough?"

Brigit gave Sibyl an inscrutable look.

"You admit that you swore?"

"Of course, stop this game. Give me the ring."

Brigit tossed it, and Sibyl caught it one-handed.

"Now release Logan."

The siren gave a piercing peacock shriek.

"Only you believe in those antiquated laws, dryad. No one witnessed our contract, so there is no deal."

"I thought you might say that."

Two crushing arms enveloped Sibyl from behind.

Chapter Eighteen
Life's Flower

ranite's form was made for muscle, not for running. He found it hard to keep up with the human as they raced down the sidewalks. Even the people all lined up along the road to see the passing parade did not slow down Logan's pace.

"Why worry about the prince?" Granite puffed. "He's a womanizer. A philanderer. Let him get what he deserves."

Logan didn't pay attention to the fae's words. Instead, he was looking frantically over and between those standing to watch the passing parade. When loud cheers started, he saw a convertible with two men go by.

His question to a young man standing at the back of the crowd confirmed it was the prince.

"Danke. Where does the parade end?"

"Past the docks, in the Fußball lot."

One of Logan's bard powers was his sweet-talking tongue, and while he preferred the truth, he didn't hesitate to bend it if needed.

"Listen," he told the man who had answered his question, "I promised my girlfriend I'd meet her at the end of the parade. If I don't get there in time, she'll be pretty mad. Maybe even break up with me. Can I use your scooter?"

The electric scooter was handed over with a good luck from the scooter's former rider and another thanks from Logan. The bard re-charged the machine with his debit card, and steered it down a side alley to avoid the crowds.

"Wait!" Granite called, but Logan didn't slow or turn. The wrestler was left standing, wondering what to do next when a woman asked, "Aren't you on the wrestling team?" She was with the man who had given Logan the scooter.

"Yes, I am," agreed Granite, asking, "Can I borrow your scooter?"

"For a kiss," she teased, giving him a saucy grin.

Granite obliged. He took her gently in an embrace and dipped her back, before giving her a kiss. His gesture got hoots from the surrounding crowd, but only a frown from the girl's companion.

Bringing her up, Granite released her and said, "Thanks!" as he grabbed her scooter and headed off after Logan.

Sam was a troll. Brigit's former roommate was an eotan like Granite, but a lumpy, half-unfinished form with a potato of a face.

He squeezed the siren harder, and Brigit cautioned him about using too much strength. "Remember, she's got hollow bones, idiot."

"She's struggling," said Sam. Each word was a heavy stone dropped from a great height, slow to arrive. "We don't want her to get away."

"Let me go!" screamed Sibyl. Despite the siren's struggles she could not break the troll's bruising grip.

Sam ignored Sibyl and addressed his remarks to Brigit. "I'm here like we agreed. This pays off my Mark of Injury. So the brownie will drop the charges?"

"Yes, yes, but only if you keep a hold of her. And don't kill her," agreed Brigit, who said to the siren, "Let Logan go, Sibyl. I'll still give you the ring, but release Logan now."

A black bird swooped down from the branches of the trees to land near them, causing Sibyl to shriek, "Attack them!"

But Sibyl's power was ineffectual, and she could not seize the bird's will.

"No can do, I'm afraid," said the crow. He hop-skipped sideways, cocking his head to observe the siren. "Sorry, lady, but we crows answer to a higher power. The Great Queen would kill us if we aided you against her grandson."

A second crow, slightly smaller, landed behind the first. He added, "Kill us? I think the Morrighan would rip our wings off while we still lived."

A third landed. It was the smallest crow yet. She croaked, "Rip our wings off, crack our beaks, and feed us alive to wolves, more like."

The three birds exchanged knowing looks.

"Yeah, so I think no-can-do," said the leader of the trio.

Sibyl sighed. "Fine, If I release Logan, this brute will let me go? And I still get the ring?"

Brigit admired the siren for still trying to bargain while she was clearly on the losing end of things. However, she still didn't like her.

"I don't care what happens to the prince," Brigit agreed. "Keep the ring and try your best."

The siren released her spell, Sam let her go, and Brigit completed two bargains with the word, "*Expletus.*"

The car with the prince was pulling in at the ballpark when Logan and Granite arrived on their scooters. Granite put his hand on Logan's shoulder to stop him as he said, "C'mon, man, you're not going to get close to him. He's protected."

Logan shrugged the hand off his shoulder and said, grimly, "I'm not going to let Sibyl get her claws into him. I like you, Granite. I really do. But the prince is human, and he deserves protection against your kind."

Leaving the scooter, Logan walked towards where the prince was standing next to an older man, who was outfitted in a bizarre costume getup that must have been for a party or something.

"I appreciate Brigit's attempt to save me," Logan said to Granite, who was following him, "even though her motivation is from an imagined debt and not because we are friends. But I owe something to the prince as a man. Not because I expect the prince to reward me. No. It's because he shouldn't suffer as I have."

After listening, Granite said, "Look, Logan, I'll help you. No, you don't owe me anything for it. But if the prince wants to hand over a juicy reward, I'm not saying no."

Relieved to have the wrestler on his side, Logan gave him a grin, saying, "Neither would I."

When the students came close to where the prince

was chatting to others, they were stopped. Logan begged the two guys in black shirts emblazoned with the word security across their chests to let him by.

"I just need one word with him? Just a quick word? It's a matter of life and death."

Before Logan could explain or grovel further, the ground under him started trembling, throwing him and the security men off-balance. At the same time Logan felt the lifting of Sibyl's spell. Reeling from the suddenness of the curse's removal, he stumbled to the ground.

On all fours, he took a deep inhalation, feeling his breath fill his lungs, his mind clear of months of fog, his spirit once more comfortable in his body. Before Logan had time to fully comprehend all the changes, a hand came under his armpit and helped him up.

The college student said, "Danke" and found himself looking into the face of the prince who was helping him regain his feet. "I did want to meet you, just not this way."

"Oh?" The prince waved back his guards, his features displaying polite interest.

"I know you don't know me, but there's a fae that is trying to Beguile you. Her name is Sibyl. She's a siren. Long blond hair. Uh. Well-developed."

Logan didn't receive the reaction he expected. The prince laughed at his warning.

"I've seen over a hundred blond-haired beauties on

the first day that I've been here."

He was a handsome man, with a careless practiced grace, and an arrogant tilt to his chin. Logan could see that getting girls would not be a problem for such a man, for even he felt the magic of that smile.

"She's going to use her fae powers to capture your attention," the college student continued, "but she's deadly. She'll curse you, tie you up in knots so hard you'll never escape her spell."

The prince gave him a pitying grin and said, "Let me guess? Ex-crazy-girlfriend, right?"

Seeing Logan's university t-shirt, he added, "A LOTTOS student, first time in Bewachterberg, right? Those fae girls can take you on a wild ride."

Logan nodded dumbly, wondering why he couldn't unstick his silver tongue. He needed to convince the prince of the siren's danger.

"Ah, college girls," the prince smiled, becoming lost in reminisces. "I can't stop them throwing themselves at me. But why would I want to? *La vie est une fleur dont l'amour est le miel.*"

From studying French in school, Logan translated the phrase even without the magic of Bewachterberg: Life is a flower of which love is the honey.

Before Logan could speak again, the older man, who had climbed out of the prince's car, was calling the royal to join him. The Prince of Bewachterberg said a goodbye, and Logan's opportunity was lost.

Granite joined him, saying, "I think we need tips from this guy. He's playing on a different level."

"That didn't quite go as planned," said Logan, sighing.

"Think on the bright side, maybe Brigit won't succeed with her plan."

"No, she succeeded. I felt Sibyl's curse lift from me when I fell to the ground."

"Oh," said Granite, "I thought you tripped because I made the earth rumble a bit. I hoped the prince wouldn't ignore a guy falling at his feet."

Logan was feeling alive, the air was fresh again, the sun was shining once more, but he couldn't help feeling a bit lost, that a bit of innocence was gone forever.

True to her word, Brigit had let Sibyl keep the ring, and it had given the siren access to the prince's hotel room without any trouble. The security guards had told her that the prince was expected to return. He would change before leaving for the evening festivities of a concert and banquet.

Sibyl arranged her naked body on the hotel room bed in a seductive pose. The corner of the bedsheet draped over one curvy hip, and her long tresses were artfully arranged to cover critical parts.

The siren wanted to make a big splash, and a quick

coupling would cement the spell she planned on casting over the prince. From the gossip she had heard, it didn't seem a naked woman in his bed would be unwelcome.

The noise of the door latch alerted. Sibyl hurriedly arranged her lip into an artful pout.

"Is this all for me?" asked the man who had entered the room. He was attractive: white-ice blond hair in a wave with humorous brown eyes. His face had a masculine maturity not seen among the young college students at LOTTOS.

Maybe this seduction wouldn't be such a chore after all.

"Certainly, if you wish it," Sibyl gave a come-hither smile.

The prince took off his sash, laying it on the dresser. He gave her a sideways smirk while he unbuttoned the cuffs of his shirt. Sibyl deliberately leaned forward, causing the sheet to slip.

"You don't seem to be the young woman I met at the tennis courts."

"She sent me in her stead. She knows how much I admire you." The siren let her voice grow husky as she brushed back a lock of hair.

Their intimate encounter was interrupted by a loud voice coming through the short hall. Clapping his hands as if it was the finale of a performance, the Chancellor emerged into the bedroom, saying, "Playtime is over."

With a sideways smile, Paul told the fae on the bed, "Too bad. I had hoped you'd come a bit later, Chancellor." The prince, who was the Doppelgänger, gave his liege a bow before leaving the two alone.

Upon the entrance of Chancellor François Auguste Bandemer, Sibyl sat straight up in bed. However, her exposed, bouncing breasts did not appeal to the only audience member remaining. Bandemer had seen far better.

"Now, my over-grasping tart, pay attention," snapped the Chancellor. "I have a banquet and an evening concert I need to prepare for. Une toilette élégante, like my own, needs the contemplation of at least two hours, if not three. So I will be brief."

Sibyl's eyes became more protuberant with each of the Chancellor's words. She began stuttering an explanation, but Bandemer raised a hand and with a wave of his magic, silenced her.

"While I freed Franco Sabbatini from your spell, but it will take at least a year for him to recover physically so I've sent him home. Your Beguiling made us lose the most important match of the year. I was put in the uncomfortable position of dining with the chancellor of our rival university and having to listen to hours of his gloating."

Recalling the humiliation, Bandemer frowned as he continued his speech.

"When I learned your plan to seduce the Prince of Bewachterberg through fae magic I was forced to act. That is an activity strictly verboten, not only by the Treaty of Sigismund but also by our honorable learning institution. For that action alone, I would need to punish you."

Bandemer caught his reflection in the room's mirror. While the silver-purple coat was eye-catching, perhaps something more classic tonight? Like the black with silver thread? Or should he go with the burgundy with pink ribbons?

He rearranged his lace cuffs as he told her, "Consider yourself expelled, my dear. The campus is barred from you. You have twenty-four hours to leave Bewachterberg before I release the griffins."

The door latch sounded again, and a woman Sibyl had never seen before entered the room. She was tall and slender, with white hair bound into a long braid. The woman wore a psychedelic shirt, faded blue jeans, and white sneakers, looking like a hip grandmother.

Perched on her shoulder was a raven the size of a human toddler.

"For my part, I'm finished. *Expletus*," said the Chancellor, symbolically wiping the palms of his hands together, "However, there is someone who has another claim upon you. Let me introduce you to Logan Dannon's grandmother. The Morrighan."

The smile of the Celtic war goddess caused Sibyl to

shrink back against the pillows. Her heart hammered.

"It seems the Morrighan arranged, behind the scenes, for her grandson to be invited to Leopold-Ottos-Universität Geheimetür to broaden his education."

Ever the showman, Bandemer gave a deep sigh and placed his right hand over his heart, his lacy cuffs fluttering with the drama of the gesture.

"While we all understand the trials and tribulations of young love, she took issue with the sucking death sentence part of the contract."

Bandemer gave himself a nod in the mirror. The black for the concert but he would alleviate its severity with a red vest.

"Bewachterberg is a peaceful country. We have no desire to be at odds with Badb Catha, the Battle Crow, a goddess in charge of sovereignty, battle sorcery, and warriors. No, indeed."

"Thank you for your call, Chancellor," said the Morrighan, her words holding a trace of an Irish accent.

"It was the least we could do. Now, I'll leave you two together to get acquainted, shall I?"

Epilogue

hat's your summer plans?" asked Logan as he took a sip of his beer. He and Brigit were having an evening at the Weberhaus, waiting for Celia to arrive.

The dryad flopped her chin down in her hand.

"Not sure. Jib wants to go backpacking across Europe. The púca wants to see some castles. What about you?"

"The folks are asking me to come home for the summer. It seems they've missed me."

"Going home sounds boring, Logan."

"Boring might be about my speed right now."

Before more could be said, Celia dropped into the seat next to Logan. Hooking her purse on her chair, she asked, "Has Granite had his set yet?"

"Nope," Brigit reassured her, while Logan added, "Plenty of time yet."

The trio had come to support the wrestler's debut. It was open mic night, and he had plans to show them a new comedy routine he was developing.

"I didn't know Granite had a sense of humor," said the naiad. "Do you think it will be a lot of locker room, guy jokes?"

"No idea," said Brigit, waving over a waiter to take their food orders now that Celia had joined them.

"How are you feeling, Logan?" asked Celia, giving him a professional survey up and down. It had been a week since the siren's spell had been lifted. His color was better, the shadows under his eyes fading.

"Pretty good, thanks to all of you."

"I'm so glad that everything worked out,' said Celia. "The gossip says that Sibyl left Geheimetür the day after the prince's parade. All her hair was gone! She was bald as a bat."

Logan was puzzled at Brigit's audible gasp to Celia's comment.

"I don't get it. Is that a fae thing?"

The dryad looked left to right before leaning over and telling Logan in a confidential manner, "When you swear fealty to the leader of your court, she cuts off a small lock of your hair. It's a symbolic gesture. It shows that the queen holds your life in her hands."

"I still don't understand."

Celia explained. "In the past, fae would fight to the death to settle their Debts of Honor. Now a token of hair means you have given your life to the one who holds it. It's the ultimate debt and can never be absolved."

Turning to Brigit, the naiad asked, "But I still don't understand how you did it, Brigit? I mean, how did you get her to leave? And what happened to the prince of Bewachterberg?"

Brigit gave a smug smile.

"I met with the Doppelgänger. We both agreed something had to be done about Sibyl."

Celia gasped, quickly adding, "So a Doppelgänger can fool both humans and fae. Even Logan's bard-sense didn't see the truth."

Logan frowned. "No, I didn't. I wonder why?"

"Because," explained the black cat, jumping onto the table, "the person Logan met at the end of the parade was the real prince."

Everyone quickly grabbed their glasses so the True Beast wouldn't knock them onto the floor.

"So Brigit made a show with Paul at the beginning of the parade, and Logan met the real prince at the end. I missed all the excitement!" complained Celia. "But was the power of the ring real?"

"Nope," Brigit told her. "Just something I found in a pawn shop. I gave it to the crows."

Celia pressed her with questions, "But, I didn't think the Doppelgänger would help without a payment?"

"I didn't have any more money…" Brigit began explaining, causing Logan to interject, "My allowance is shot. Thank you very much."

Brigit made a face at the human before continuing, "So I bartered."

Celia's eyes widened. "You didn't -?" and when the dryad didn't answer, the naiad continued with an awed whisper, "I guess that it wouldn't be too much of a sacrifice. A lover who can be anyone you can imagine…"

Logan's shocked blue eyes meet Brigit's brown ones. "I hope you didn't."

"I don't sleep with beings just for you, Logan Dannon. I sleep with who I want. When I want."

"You didn't answer my question," said Celia, rather urgently, but the lights were starting to dim. The noise on the stage indicated the first set was beginning, and it looked like Granite was going to be the first one up.

After the eotan's first joke was meet with utter silence from the audience, Logan murmured to Jib, "Was that supposed to be funny? Did I miss the punchline?"

The cat, needing the last word, replied, "Yes and no."

Author Notes

I hope you enjoyed the first of four planned books in the College Fae series. Each book will cover one year of college.

I love reading your comments on Amazon or Goodreads. Your review doesn't need to be long - even a line or two makes a difference in helping others discover new books.

As a personal thank you, **find a short story preview: *Knight of Cups*** featuring the characters of Jib and Brigit from *Never Date a Siren* right after the glossary for this book.

Do you love free stories? Find them at www.ByrdNash.com with a behind-the-scenes look at my writing, reviews pf other fantasy books, and giveaways. I also provide opportunities to become beta readers or to obtain ARC's (Advanced Reader Copies) of my books prior to release.

www.ByrdNash.com

Glossary

ABOUT THE COUNTRY

Bewachterberg
German for "Hidden/Guarded Mountain."
A country located south of Germany, similar in
history and tradition to Bavaria. However, due to the
Treaty of Sigismund, the country kept its sovereignty.

Geheimetür
German for "Secret Door."
A university town located in Bewachterberg.

Treaty of Sigismund
In 1890, after being told by a Cassandra about his
country's future, the King of Bewachterberg signed a
treaty with the fae to hide the country for 99 years
and a day.

**Leopold-Ottos-Universität Geheimetür,
Bewachterberg** (German)
or **Leopold Otto University** (English)
Affectionately called LOTTOS, was founded by the
royal family in 1521. Once a monastery, the holy

brothers were removed during the Protestant Reformation in 1521.

The University is managed by a Rector (traditionally a human) and in ceremonies is lead by a Chancellor (traditionally a fae, often related to the royal line of Bewachterberg).

About the Chancellor's haute couture

François Auguste Bandemer follows the seasonal wear established by Louis XIV of France (1638-1715). Summer fashion season begins on Pentecost (the seventh Sunday after Easter, about mid- to late-May). Spring wear (*été*) might include parasols, face masks, and fans, and uses lightweight silks.

The Winter (*hiver*) season begins on November 1, All Saint's Day, and includes velvet and satin with furs, capes, and muffs.

FAE CULTURE

Perilous Realm

The faerie world is composed of many kingdoms, just as the Human Lands has many countries. Each kingdom is ruled by a queen who is equal in status (theoretically) to all the other queens. However, in reality courts differ in status due to size, magical ability, and political strength.

Fae

(plural or singular, the word fae remains the same) -
beings that call the Perilous Realm their home. All fae
are generally twice as strong as their human
counterparts.

Three things define a Fae being's world: their sworn
loyalty to the queen of their royal court; their Sept (or
clan); and Affiliation (magic source).

Beings

The preferred term to describe another fae.

Bondmates

Instead of using the term "friends," the fae use
bondmates to denote the complicated ties that form
their network of companions. Debts and exchanges in
the Laws of Civility let others test each others mettle,
deeming them worthy or not, due to how they
respond.

Affiliations

Fae magical abilities are from seven affiliations: Wood,
Metal, Stone, Water, Wind, Flame, and Time/Memory.
It is possible for a fae to have more than one
affiliation but there is always one that is dominant.

Laws of Civility

All kingdoms acknowledge a code of behavior called the Laws of Civility, however enforcement is a nebulous, free-flowing, every-fae-for-themselves, process. Humans are outside of this system, as they are not seen as worthy participants.

Debts of Honor

Something owed, acknowledged between both parties. There are many different types but the one Brigit owes Logan in Never Date a Siren is a Debt of Gratitude. How a fae handles, incurs, and manages their Debts is how they form relationships with others as it provides proof of your integrity (or lack thereof).

Fiat of Harm/Injury

An official and binding declaration against another. Brigit declares two Fiats: one against the Bog Sprites for attempting to drug her, and another against Sibyl for attempted murder. A lesser form of this would be a Mark of Injury.

Expletus

The formal word used by a debt-holder to acknowledge the debt is at an end.

FAE SEPTS (Clans)

Septs

Clans of the fae are grouped by type. It can influence allegiances as those of the same clan feel familiar to each other.

True Beast

A fae that presents physically as an animal and cannot change into a human form.

Shapeshifters

Fae who can transform from animal to human form and back again. While they appear human, their beast side plays a large part in their personality.

Beguilers

Fae who ensnare humans through their voice, song, or physical appearance. Beguiling is usually fatal to the beguiled. Beguiling powers do not work between fae, only upon humans.

- **Siren** - a shapeshifter associated with birds, having wings, bird feet, and a bird's tail. Affiliation: wind.
- **Kelpie** - also called Each Uisage (Gaelic), bäckahäst or bækhest (Scandavianian), Ceffyl

Dwr (Welsh). Water horse that typically ensnares humans which they then proceed to drown. Affiliation: water.

Naturals

Keep to a human form, and are closely connected to natural materials found in the human world. Think trees, streams, rocks, and mountains.

- **Dryad** - a fae being associated with trees, usually affiliated with wood.
- **Naiad** - a fae being associated with springs and rivers, usually affiliated with water.
- **Eotan** - beings with supernatural strength. Contains giants, trolls, dwarves. Usually affiliated with stone or metal.

The Kindly Ones

A branch of fae who like to help humans. Because they have a long history with the Human Lands, they are immune to iron. Beware though, they can be turned to a darker side through poor usage (see trickster/boggart).

- **Brownie** - also called broonie, brùnaidh (Scottish Gaelic) with other England and Scotland variations including hobs, silkies, and ùruisgs, bwbach (Welsh) and fenodryee (Manx).

Tricksters

A Sept, self-described. Many are True Beasts (horses, cats, dogs), although others are shapeshifters and appear in various forms, sometimes human. Magical affiliations vary greatly.

- **Púca** - a mischievous creature, commonly found in animal form (such as cat, dog, or horse). They can cross over to be a Beguiler or a boggart. They can also be True Beasts or shapeshifters.

- **Boggart** - malevolent spirits causing mischief (i.e. losing socks, milk going sour, horse going lame). A Kindly One can be transformed into a boggart, or a boggart can be from the countryside and be attached to a place (genius loci).

  Those inhabiting the countryside are often more dangerous. For instance, they will abduct children to their death. Common nicknames include bug, bugbear, bogey, bogun, bogeman, bogle, and the Old English terms, pūcel, or Irish púca, or Welsh bwg.

Time/Memory Affiliated Groups

- **Cassandra** - referring to a being who has prophetic powers. As a crossover power, a Cassandra can be from many Septs, or even a human. Logan's cousin, Evelyn, is a Cassandra (see my other book, *The Wicked Wolves of Windsor and other fairytales*).

- **Doppelgänger** - (German usage is capitalized, same form in plural as singular). They hold the highest form of fae power - Mindbending (the affiliation of time and memory). It is believed that nine Doppelgänger hailing from the courts signing the Treaty of Sigismund, used magic to hide Bewachterberg for 99 years and a day.

HUMAN LANDS

Human Lands

Self-explanatory.

The Morrighan

An Irish Goddess who goes by several names. As the Morrighan, The Great Queen, Queen of the Dead, Queen of Phantoms - is affiliated with land rule, sovereignty and queenship. As Badb Catha (the Battle Crow), she is aligned with the otherworld powers of battle and battle sorcery, warriors and bloodshed, as well as prophecy. Other names and aspects include Macha (earth and fertility), and Némain (which has a more hazy meaning, but could be related to battle frenzy).

Snowden

(Old English meaning "snow hill"). Yr Wyddfa, is the highest mountain in Wales. The Welsh name means "the barrow" (a funeral cairn). It has a long folklore history of being attached to King Arthur legend. Folklore states if you sleep on the mountain, you would either go insane, become a poet, or never wake again.

Genius Loci

A being/spirit attached to specific place.

The **Scottish Lullaby** that the brownie sings to Logan is *Do chuirfinnse fèin.*

Sudden Death Chukker - in Polo, a chukker is a time of play lasting about 7 minutes. After six chukkers, if the match is a tie, there is a short intermission before a final match. In a Sudden Death Chukker whichever team scores first breaks the tie and wins.

Tulpa

A magically created being developed by powerful thoughts or fears, deliberate or not. The being eventually becomes sentient and relatively autonomous of its creator. The closet monster and under-the-bed monster are examples of Tulpa.

Wraith

A sentient ghost of a human which can act independently of its history and timeline. Wraith's differ from other ghosts, shades, and haunts, as they are formed from humans who have died in the Perilous Realm.

The Knight of Cups

A magical fae adventure
featuring Jib and Brigit
(Preview)

First Night

Brigit Cullen didn't like the forest. Being a fae dryad, she knew when things didn't feel right, and these trees were all wrong.

"Stop bouncing around so much, I'm trying to sleep back here," said the cat she was carrying in her backpack.

"Excuse me, Jib!" the woman snapped back at her companion, "But if you hadn't told off the driver, we wouldn't be taking a cross country hike."

Poking its head up, the black cat dislodged the knapsack flap. The fae being climbed partially out, placing its front paws on Brigit's shoulders to meow in her pointed ear.

"I was simply correcting that poor human's belief that I was a cute kitty. I'm a dangerous púca Trickster. He should be grateful I didn't set him on fire for the insult he gave me."

Like all True Beasts, Jib was far more massive than its form promised. The púca felt as heavy as a bowling bowl. Brigit bounced the pack up, to give her lower back some relief. Jib yowled a protest, causing Brigit to snarl, "Well, genius, we would already be at the hostel if it weren't for you."

Both of them were feeling out of sorts. The summer was almost at an end and, while touring had been fun, Brigit was ready to be back home in Geheimetür.

After completing her first school year at Leopold-Ottos-Universität Geheimetür, in Bewachterberg, the two fae had toured Italy and France. Using her dryad healing skills among the vineyards padded Brigit's purse, but she was ready to be back among her friends and with a regular schedule.

Being on the road, sleeping in strange trees, and without regular meals had made them both cranky. The fall semester would begin in just a few weeks, but Jib insisted on a detour.

Now they were lost in an unfriendly forest with the late summer sun setting in a bank of what looked to be stormy clouds.

"If you didn't insist we visit a castle, I could already be sleeping in a tree," she told the cat, adding, "and saving my money."

"You are so stingy, princess. Who taught you that? It wasn't your mother. The queen appreciates the finer things in life as I do," replied the púca.

As a member of her parents' court in the Perilous Realm, Jib had known the dryad since birth. Sometimes this long familiarity made Brigit resent the fae Trickster.

She had run away from the Perilous Realm to attend LOTTOS, only for Jib to rat out her location. After she was discovered, the True Beast negotiated an agreement with her parents that if the púca chaperoned Brigit, she could stay in the human lands.

This arrangement, made without her input, numbered first in her list of resentments. Thinking upon this, the dryad muttered, "Jailer."

Jib ignored her remark, meowing plaintively, "Just because I've never slept in a human castle doesn't mean I need to. I'll return to school and tell all of our friends about sleeping in ditches and under mushrooms."

"Okay! Okay! I get it. Your life is nothing but suffering. Enough already."

After their spat, the two continued in silence for about half an hour as the cloud cover increased. A slight mist started to make everything damp.

"Talk to a tree, Brigit," begged the cat. Many púca, especially kelpies, loved water. However, Jib, with its magical fire affiliation, couldn't stand being wet. "Ask it where to go. Don't be a contrary boggart."

"I'm not talking to these trees. There's something

off about them."

Jib retreated further into the bag letting the flap cover its head. Round orange eyes peered out surveying the dark shadows around them.

"Now that you mention it, they do look rather unpleasant. Too much moss and rot. Diseased, huh?"

"Old," replied Brigit, but before she could expound on the subject, she cried out in surprise, "a road!"

The two emerged onto a paved drive. Looking down the wide lane, they could see peaked roofs silhouetted against the darkening sky.

"Castle!" Jib purred in excitement.

Seeing a possible end to their long journey, Brigit quickened her step.

When they reached the house, she contradicted Jib's description.

"Not a castle, Jib, though it's pretty big, isn't it? I'm guessing a French château. Baroque or French Gothic. Something like that. I get the human history periods mixed up."

"Looks like a falling down pile to me. Perfect mouse hunting territory."

The two were standing in front of a monster of a building. The French château boasted four distinct levels with rows and rows of tall narrow windows. It had a sharply peaked roof, and Brigit counted four turrets.

Though the place was old and historical, it was also in disrepair. The six visible chimney stacks were towering things, but one was crooked like a drunkard, and none spouted any smoke. Shingles seemed to be missing, as well as some window glass, but the darkening gloom made it hard to discern the extent of the damage.

The two walked up the steps, Brigit stepping over the broken masonry and where tree roots cracked through the stonework. Feeling the dryad was moving too slow, the excited púca jumped down from Brigit's shoulders to trot up the handrail.

As Brigit reached the door, she saw an engraved brass plaque, now mostly green mounted on the wall to the side. Bending close, she read aloud, "Château du Puis."

"Castle of the grotto spring," translated the cat, who was a host of stray knowledge about human ways.

"Don't think anyone is here, but let's see." As she knocked on the massive French wood doors, Brigit warned her companion, "Remember to keep your smart mouth shut. You've already landed us into one pickle already. Right now, I'm tired, hungry, and this sprinkle is about to turn into a downpour."

Before Brigit could give the True Beast another caution, the door opened.

"Oh, *Salut.* About time you got here. We've been holding dinner for hours," said a teen girl, dressed in modern clothes: a simple short-sleeved, purple t-shirt with a scoop neck, faded blue jeans, and sneakers.

As the two stared at each other, the girl pushed a pair of round glasses up her nose. Her hair was partially blond, but mostly it was colored robin's egg blue.

Someone called from deeper in the house and the girl at the door yelled back over her shoulder, "It's a short, black girl. Yes, I'm bringing her!"

The teen turned back to Brigit, telling her, "Hurry up and come in. Dinner will get cold otherwise. Besides, it's best not to be out in the park when the sun goes down. Things roam about which you do not want to meet."

With official permission to enter, Jib jumped over the threshold, quickly disappearing down a dim corridor without a goodbye. Brigit whispered under her breath, "Rude, as usual."

After the girl closed the pair of front doors, she locked them and beckoned the dryad to follow her, saying, "I'm starving, what about you?"

"The same," agreed Brigit, whose nose was already sniffing out the rich aromas floating down the hallway. Her stomach growled. "I'm a vegetarian, though."

"That's fine. There's soup, bread, fruit, so I'm sure there is something for you."

The front hall had dim lighting, but Brigit had keen eyesight. The decline from outside was repeated in the château's interior. The square fade marks on the wood paneling were evidence that paintings were missing. There were broken wall brackets, a bench missing a leg sat crookedly against the wall, and the warped wood parquet floor crackled under their feet.

The couple entered a dining hall that was probably sumptuous in its heyday but was now worse than tired. As a dryad, Brigit could mentally touch organic materials: the moldy mutters from the long window curtains almost made her gag.

It would be a courtesy to end their suffering by burning them. Hopefully, far away from anyone breathing.

The only thing well cared for was a massive oak table that could seat twenty dominating the room. The wood smelled of lemon and the candelabra of polished silver, with little tarnish, held lit candles. Brigit's fingertips touched the tabletop in reverence, and the furniture replied in a majestic tone: *I prepare and serve.*

One of the dinner guests was a well-dressed, polished woman, older than Brigit by at least a dozen years. Her makeup was immaculate, and not a hair would have dared to be out of place. Her expensive clothes were quick to tell the dryad their worth with a sneer: *you could never afford us.*

The woman addressed the teenager in cultivated French.

"Introduce us, Camille."

"My father, Hugh Dupuis and his lover, Lorraine Bonnet," said Camille, indicating the man at the head of the table and the woman. She showed Brigit a seat.

The chair was heavy and old, maybe even older than the table. The dryad could feel the dry rot and wormwood in it.

Will you hold my weight?

Surely, jeune fille, said the chair. *I serve this cursed household until the end.*

Brigit was doubtful of its ability to fulfill its promise but figured if she fell on her butt, she would still get something to eat.

"I apologize for my daughter," said the man, unfolding a cloth napkin and placing it in his lap. He had narrow shoulders, a long neck with a prominent Adam's apple, and high cheekbones that enhanced the shadows of his face in the candlelight. His ski-jump nose provided a long view to look down upon someone, especially someone as short as Brigit.

"Brigit Cullen," she introduced herself.

She was greeted by a long silent gaze from three sets of eyes before Camille's father rang a silver handbell located at the side of his plate. At the ring, a door at the end of the dining hall opened.

A butler, wearing traditional black and white,

entered, carrying a hammered brass bowl about the size of a soup tureen. The presentation had such pomp and circumstance, Brigit couldn't wait to see what was inside; she hoped it was the promised soup.

The servant handed the bowl to Camille's father, who took it in both hands as it was quite heavy. Next, the dish was passed to the woman at his right, who held it only a moment. When Camille received the bowl, she stood up and brought it to Brigit.

As the dryad received the dish, she looked down and was surprised to see the bowl contained only clear water. Bright wasn't sure what to do next but when Camille's father held out his hands, she passed the object to him.

He raised it over his head and said in a reverent tone, "The Blessed Bowl."

There was a long pause before the bowl was returned to the butler. The servant placed it on the table and left. In a moment he returned again, but this time he carried a short sword.

The butler walked clockwise around the table three times, holding the blade at its hilt with point down. Finally, he stopped and handed the sword's hilt to Camille's father. Bowing to the sword, he left the room.

"The Arming Sword," declared Hugh Dupuis, before laying it in the middle of the table, its hilt at his plate, the point towards where the bowl sat.

Everyone stared at the sword in silence, all except the dryad. She was giving a side-eye to the medieval knight who had appeared behind Camille's father. He wore chain mail and armor over his arms and legs. A sleeveless surcoat flowed to his knees and a wide leather belt was buckled at his waist.

Brigit wouldn't embarrass anyone by commenting upon the ghost. Humans could be touchy about such things.

Besides, the first course was arriving and the dryad was really hungry.

Visit **www.ByrdNash.com**
to read the entire short story!

Acknowledgments

To get a book from rough draft to completion takes many people who provide support and advice with nothing in return. Often these people may go without their praises being sung.

During the development of this book, I had some amazing helpers providing me invaluable feedback. Specifically Andie K., who lent me German assistance and suggestions (above and beyond the call of duty, and holding me through multiple drafts), and Laurie H. whose eagle-eyed and detailed notes helped me improve the consistency of the story.

Other beta readers who have been with me from the beginning: Astrid M., and Jessica F., were the best cheerleading squad any author could desire. Both have been invaluable as a support team for me.

Kate H. once again caught my typos, verb abuse, and prompted me to rewrite sentences or scenes that needed clarity.

Just know this author greatly appreciates all the reading all of you did and advice you provided.

CPSIA information can be obtained
at www.ICGtesting.com
Printed in the USA
LVHW040614171219
640671LV00009B/490/P

9 781733 456630